OZ

IS BURNING

Also from B Cubed Press

Alternative Truths

More Alternative Truths: Tales from the Resistance

After the Orange: Ruin and Recovery

Alternative Theology

Digging Up My Bones,

by Gwyndyn T. Alexander

Firedancer,

by S.A. Bolich

Alternative Apocalypses

OZ is Burning

Edited by
Phyllis Irene Radford

Cover Design
Bob Brown

Published by

B Cubed Press
Kiona, WA

Copyright

Editor's Foreword

Phyllis Irene Radford

As the year turned toward a new decade and new hope for better times, news erupted from Australia. The entire continent was on fire. Even with the Pacific Ocean and a hemisphere separating me from this tragedy. The news flashed around social media with horrific pictures of animals badly burned, habitat destroyed, and nearly a billion of them lost forever.

Internet friends related their own stories of destruction and the need to evacuate. The city of Canberra is supposed to have the best air quality in the world. It was so smothered in smoke that friends had to evacuate or risk serious damage to fragile lungs and hearts.

And the days of engulfing fires turned into weeks, turned into a month, or more.

Relief came eventually in the form of rain. The fires died, but there was no longer ground cover to absorb the lashing water from the skies. Floods followed.

Then COVID 19 sent the entire world into quarantine. 2020 no longer offered hope of being a better year.

The animals and habitat devastated by the fires are still there.

Australian authors were also hit hard by the multiple body slams of life interrupted. Book buying fell off.

And so my friends in Australia suggested over closed writer forums that someone create an anthology featuring Australian authors might help with money and exposure of the plight of their home to the wider world. I have direct access to B-Cubed Press having edited four anthologies and several books for them in three years.

All of B-Cubed Press's publications donate a share to a charity, usually ACLU because we were born in political satire in January 2017. For this anthology, we are donating a share of the profits and my editor's share to WIRES, NSW Wildlife Information, Rescue and Education Service Inc. https://www.wires.org.au/donate/emergency-fund

Life is a mixed bag of tragedy, laughter, and hope. The stories are just as mixed. All of them touched me. I hope you find them enlightening.

Thus *OZ IS BURNING* was born.

Phyllis Irene Radford
Welches, Oregon USA
May 2020

P.S. the spelling in this book may be eccentric to US standards, but most Australians abide by UK preferences.

Table of Contents

And Gaia Screams...

Ann Poore

"And Gaia Screams" attempts to express the anger, grief, and sadness felt driving through many drought and fire affected areas of Australia.

The poem started out as part of a suite of songs written for a heavy metal project. The project never went anywhere, but the poems remain...

Ann Poore

And Gaia Screams...
by
Ann Poore

(...Unheard, unseen,
Unseen, unheard...)
In bitter dreams
Again She sees
The greedy flames
Her lungs on fire
Her body burnt.
There's no escape
The pain She feels.
Her temples razed,
Her daughters raped.
Her children fall,
And then they're gone.
There's no appeal-
No one to face
Her fear and rage.
All are dis-eased,
And then erased,
Devoured by greed.
Her spirit bleeds,
And She is lost.
And Gaia screams
And screams again.

Across the Ditch

Clare Rhoden

This story is inspired by the ships of the Australian Navy who rescued locals and holiday makers from endangered coastal towns along the east coast of Australia during the Black Summer bushfires of 2019-2020.

People and pets were transported to the safety of Victoria's capital city Melbourne. It was many weeks until everyone could return to the fire-grounds to collect their cars or inspect the damage to their homes.

Clare Rhoden

Across the Ditch
by
Clare Rhoden

Noelle leans on the railing and turns her binoculars towards the shore.

She doesn't need binoculars to see the fire, but the simple act of lifting her hands up to eye level makes her feel more official. Makes her look more calm. The postcard picture of a commander in charge of a Navy vessel.

Because her disruptive pattern uniform–that journalists call a camouflage grey jumpsuit–with tabs of rank on the shoulders and honour patches on the chest is not reassuring enough for civilians. She must seem to be doing something, even though everyone knows that she can learn nothing new through the glasses, nothing that wasn't confirmed before all the comms dropped out.

She's keeping busy because she knows, like everyone else, that there is nothing they can do. There is nothing left, and no way back. The entire shoreline is glowing, great crowns of flame bursting skywards, cresting along the fire's bulk like a new horizon, an overblown after-image of the day's bloody sunset.

The fiery dusk is gone, but the conflagration on the shore keeps expanding. They are a kilometre out at sea, and they can feel the heat on their faces, searing like a million blowtorches in concert. The back-lit air writhes with glowing ashes, flying soot. Through her binoculars, Noelle sees solid black specks rising and then dropping straight down. Bird-shaped specks. She lowers the glasses and turns around.

Immediately behind her, a clutch of wide-eyed passengers is flanked by sailors looking similarly stunned. She blinks a couple of times, trying to clear her vision before remembering that it's the air that's thick and grainy, not her eyesight.

She frowns at one of the sailors. "Leading Seaman Jones, report!"

"Captain!"

Noelle nods permission for him to continue. Jones has a round, soft face, sullied with dirt and sweat. The scorching offshore wind flaps his hi-vis vest around him like the wings of a panicked crow.

"Lower decks secured, Captain. Water and food sufficient for forty-eight hours. At current numbers, that is."

Their eyes catch, but they don't say aloud that they may need to pluck more refugees from the dreadful shore, or drag anyone else out of the pitching waves.

"The animals?" A question she never thought she'd ask, but she never thought to use her destroyer for bushfire rescues either.

"All secure, captain."

That's fifteen dogs, seven cats, and one pet rabbit in a padded carrier. One of the lower decks is now a holding pen, with crates of tinned food and pallets of bottled water dividing off sections.

The best thing about the animals is that their people stay with them and don't crowd her on deck. Which means that Noelle will be heading down there to share her decision. She raises one hand to shoulder height.

"Crew of *HMAS Ginan*," she begins. "Passengers." She waits until the muffled murmurs and whimpers on deck disappear beneath the roar of the gale.

"As you know, we've been tracking down the east coast for more than a month. We've found no safe haven, and we've received no communication for several days. I have therefore decided to leave this shore."

"What? No! We want to go home!"

"There is no home, you fools!" says Leading Seaman Jones, sparking further outcries.

Noelle waits until relative quiet returns. "Sorry, Captain," mumbles Jones.

Noelle nods. "We are going to cross the Tasman," she announces. "Nobody can say what the future holds, but what we all need now is a little taste of New Zealand."

Passengers and crew look at each other.

"I've always wanted to visit New Zealand," says an older man at the back of the crowd.

Noelle laughs, a rasping sound. "Looks like you get your wish."

OZ is Burning

"Burn! Burn! BURN!"

Alma Alexander

I simply watched in disbelief, listened with appalled horror at the piling statistics. The hundreds of thousands of acres, of habitat, going up in smoke—of the people on the beaches, standing against a blood red sky, in darkness while the clock insisted it was morning—the smoke and the darkness and the ashes falling—and I did what I usually do, the only thing I CAN do. I turned it into words. This story.

Alma Alexander

"Burn! Burn! BURN!"
by
Alma Alexander

"Wait! Stop!" Gaia reached out to gather a gasping koala into her arms, looked up into a sky which was an improbable shade of dark red and empty of birds. "What are you doing? Who are you?"

"I am Flame," said the other, and fire danced in the eyes that Gaia saw turned towards her. A fire that was fueled by hatred and madness, by something broken, driven beyond endurance. "What am I doing?" Flame continued, baring his teeth in a rictus that might have been intended as a smile. It was, frighteningly, not. "They asked for this. THEY ASKED. They didn't care. Now they will care. They will remember. If they live, they will remember."

Gaia, now clutching two koalas and with a half-grown kangaroo clinging to her leg, stared down to where a ring of fire was irrevocably sweeping down the curve of the land. Down it swept to the sea, down to the beach where now a clutch of hollow-eyed humans, trying to breathe through filter masks, milled about aimlessly at the water's edge. They stood in the ocean while it lapped at their knees, or hunkered down on fragile-looking boats that floated on a sea that was turned to blood by the red light all around them.

"What did they do to you?" Gaia gasped.

"Individually? Probably nothing," Flame spat. "Collectively? They're a disease. Humans are a VIRUS. I don't see YOU grabbing any of them, do I?"

A singed kookaburra sat on Gaia's shoulder, silent. Against Gaia's cheek its feathers were rough with grit, leaving smears from smudged wings stained with smoke. From somewhere beyond their circle of vision, out in the smoky murk, an animal screamed. Gaia flinched. "They too are the children of..."

A creature came lurching from out of the smoky haze, a chimera made out of half a dozen different animals. In the land which was home to something like a duck-billed platypus that didn't seem too outlandish, perhaps–but this beast carried bits from a much wider range of creatures. It had parts that had once belonged to a polar bear. To a lion. To an orangutan. To giraffe. To a rhino. To a turtle. To a snow leopard. To a condor. To a butterfly. To a bee.

When it spoke, its voice was unintelligible, a confused mix of sounds—chirps, grunts, whistles, whispers, groans, roars, something that almost approached something human but never quite made it. Its words, instead, echoed with clarity inside the mind.

"We are all the children," the ChymerBeast said. "They changed the climate. They took the habitat. They decided that our horns or our bones or our hides were useful as aphrodisiacs, or snake-oil medicine, or whatever they felt like wanting at the moment. It did not matter that they slaughtered the whole beast to cut off its horn–or a vital living animal so that they could stick its hide on their floors, or its head on their wall. It did not matter that they leveled forests for palm oil and left the wildlife to starve in the burned-out husks left behind. All that mattered was THEIR wants, THEIR needs."

Gaia looked around at the animals gathered in her arms, at her feet. "But these are dying now..."

"Yes," Flame said, snarling. "Scour. Scour it all. Cleanse. Clean. Let there be purity again. Let the disease disappear. Life is a liability. Let life go away. Let it burn. Let it all burn. We will drive them all into the sea."

A voice came, a voice that sounded like it came from under water, distant, yet present in the smoke and murk.

A new voice spoke.

"The sea? You would drive them into the sea? The sea that is dying already, long before you decided to burn the land clean?"

Gaia found her hands wet, dripping with salt water, holding a piece of bleached dead coral in her fingers. It was sharp; it cut her fingertips, and her blood welled out of the cuts, left dark red trails where it fell and snaked down in tiny scarlet rivulets guided by the coral's uneven surface. With a cry of pain, Gaia opened her hand and dropped the coral branch; it fell at her feet, in the dust and ashes, lying there white and red and accusing.

"I am Moana, I am the sea," the voice said. "The sea that is being destroyed by the change in pH, by increasing warmth, by pollution. They have taken my riches and wonders and they have made them into processed foods; they disrupt the cycles of my life, my currents, my depths and my shallows—they drill on the ocean floors for their precious oil and they care not where the fallout goes–they drain the sea of porpoises and narwhals and whales and tuna and halibut and cod and they leave it filled with algal blooms, with oil slicks, and with jellyfish. It used to be that humans could wade in and swim in the cobalt waters that welcomed them. Now they have to wade through drifting plastic garbage to get into deeper waters and there's a gyre in the ocean big enough to be called a continent; there are flesh-eating bugs in the shallows, and there are places where the ocean is brown, not blue any more. And then they watch the great icebergs calve off the vanishing ice, and all that cold fresh water comes pouring into the salt of my waters, and everything changes. They pour waste and radioactivity into me. They blame me, for my levels rising, for being the mother of storms they have never seen the like of before… and they never look in the mirror, they never see themselves behind it all…"

Gaia was weeping softly. "I loved them," she said, sobbing. "I did, I loved them—I loved them all–where did you all come from, who hated them so? Why are you here to punish and to mete out death and destruction…? Who ARE you?"

Flame gazed back at her, and behind the fire in his eyes there was something… something else… something that made Gaia choke on her own breath. Something that was… that was PITY.

"You must have seen it, in those humans you love so," Flame said. "In the wake of great tragedy, great trauma, things that nobody and nothing should be expected to experience and survive and understand... they don't stay whole. They fracture. They become different entities, who can then do, individually, the things that are necessary for the original whole individual to endure and stay alive. You broke, Gaia. THEY broke you. We... we are you. We are those parts of you that now need to put aside your compassion, and your grace, and your bounty. We are the vengeance. We are what's left. We are the vaccine to a deadly disease. We are here to cure. We are here to make it right again."

"You are killing them," Gaia whispered.

"If that is what it takes for them to understand," Flame said. "Yes. We will do that. I will, and my brother Flood will, and my sister Hurricane will, and all those others. All they have ever known is love, YOUR love. Now it's time to teach them that love has an end."

Gaia was silent, her eyes closed tight, fat tears squeezing out from between her eyelashes, rolling down her cheeks, falling into the dust at her feet.

Somewhere on Earth, it began to rain.

Red Sky at Morning

Sue Bursztynski

One evening in January 2020, while I was on my way home from a visit, a dramatic storm broke, making me take shelter in a favourite restaurant. It was too hot to cook, anyway, so I ordered dinner. I got talking with the lady at the next table, who told me she had been with her mother in a small town on the south coast of New South Wales, on New Year's Eve. The town was lucky to have escaped the fires, but roads were closed and supplies short. And the sky that day was...red. She showed me some photos on her phone, of the landscape before and after. "Like Mars, isn't it?" she said.

My story was born.

Sue Bursztynski

OZ is Burning

Red Sky at Morning
by
Sue Bursztynski

The red lunchtime sky on New Year's Eve looked like the sky of Mars. Selena was trying to focus on *The War Of The Worlds* for Year 9 English, assuming school was starting any time soon. The bushfires had bypassed her small town, but the roads were blocked and supplies were short.

Selena had posted photos of the before and after landscape to Instagram. "It's Mars here!" she told her followers. "I'm reading *The War Of The Worlds* for school and every time I see this, I watch out for Martian machines."

Giving up reading for the moment, she went to the window and gazed out at the bright sky, wondering if the next thing she'd see would be red Martian weeds. Then she sighed and went upstairs to change the linen in the guests' rooms.

There were several guests right now, all of them journalists here to cover the fires, no tourists. Most of the journalists in town now were staying in its one hotel, but a few had preferred the small Koala Lodge bed and breakfast run by Selena's mother.

They left early every day. Thank goodness, communications were not out. They were in contact both with their papers or stations and with colleagues in other towns nearby. The helicopters that were dropping supplies were also filming fires from above.

"Just as well," her favourite guest, a photographer called Tom, had said as he left that morning. "There's only so much we can report about one small place that hasn't even been destroyed, but none of us is going anywhere for a while."

"You could hitch a ride on a helicopter," she suggested.

"Too many of us. Besides, as long as there's a story..." He grinned. "There's a lot of competition. If we went home, I guarantee someone who stayed would get a sudden scoop after we left."

Three more guests came down the stairs, two dark young men and a blonde woman. Despite their names, James, George and Jill, they had a foreign accent she didn't recognise. They were the last arrivals and were sharing the B and B's family room. She had had a lot of chats with them over breakfast, though mostly small talk. They smiled, but didn't say much. Still, she liked them. They gave a friendly wave as they went out the door.

"Have a good day!" Selena called.

"Have a good day where, I wonder?" Tom murmured. "I haven't seen them anywhere near where the rest of us go. At the pub at lunchtime, yes, but..." He shrugged. "I'd love to know how they got here, with all those blocked roads. I don't even know who sent them. They just go off into the bush on foot. Who are they even going to interview out there? Well, I'd better be going. Lots of photos and videos to take—and there is quite a spectacular sky today!"

It was still spectacular, though for all the wrong reasons, Selena thought as she flicked the last sheet on the final bed in the family room. That sky reminded everyone that not only was the bush burning, not only homes, but animals were being destroyed. Those that survived were losing *their* homes. Who needed a Martian invasion?

We did all this to ourselves, she thought. *It's too easy to blame someone, anyone else for your troubles*. She went downstairs, wondering when Mum was coming home. Her mother was off scraping together supplies. There was not much left in the supermarket, and the community centre, which had been sorting the helicopter drops, was giving priority to individuals and families over business.

Selena texted Mum. "Going for a walk. Let me know if u need me."

The air quality was poor, according to the EPA website, so she put on a respirator mask—she and Mum were running low on those too.

She missed her friends Thando and Dylan, both off on holiday. Dylan's family were in Melbourne, away from the worst of the smoke. Thando had gone there to visit an uncle, before the roads were blocked. Her mother, a nurse at the local hospital, was needed here. They were Zimbabwean, and as Thando's mother, Marisa, had said, they had come here because a regional town *had* to be peaceful!

It wasn't far to where the first of the journalists and photographers were working, but Selena wore boots and her backpack with water and lunch. There was a lot of rubbish and ash underfoot, though the trees were unburned.

She waved at a newspaper reporter sitting on a folding chair, interviewing a grimy, exhausted firefighter who was on break. A photographer was snapping away. There was a team from a local TV station filming a young woman telling her audience about the latest dramas, commenting on the unusual sky. Selena heard her say, "Just like Mars!" and grinned.

She was well into the bush before seeing anyone she knew. Tom was waiting with his camera while his reporters discussed their next presentation.

"Hi, Tom, how's it going?" Selena asked.

"Not bad. I got some shots of that sky, and there's someone giving scorched animals water. We're waiting for the vets. I can't wait to get out of this smoke. Why are *you* out of the house when you don't have to be?"

Selena shrugged. "Oh, just getting some photos for Instagram. My friends will want to see what's happening. Have you seen Jill, James and George?"

Tom waved. "I think they went that-a-way. Not sure how far... or why. Be careful, though, there are some trees that look a bit shaky in this wind."

"I will." She had been walking several minutes without encountering anyone at all when she heard a tree crashing and an agonised yell. The sound must have been loud enough to be heard from a fair distance; several people came running. Selena hurried on in that direction.

James was lying on the ground, groaning, a heavy tree branch across his leg. He was alone, but Selena had all guests' phone numbers. She also had Marisa's number. If Marisa was nearby, she could at least give first aid.

"What is it, Selena? I'm on my way home from my shift... Oh. All right, I'll be there soon."

Some of the other journalists laid their equipment on the ground to help remove the branch. Marisa was hurrying towards him. "Careful!" she called. "Wait till I get there. You might make it worse. One of you call an ambulance."

"Already done, Marisa," said Tom.

"Then you should have waited till they arrived," she grumbled. "It's dangerous! Never mind now... Move, please."

She knelt beside the injured man. "Let me look at you. I don't think we've met. I'm Marisa. I'm a nurse."

She reached gently for his leg.

"No!" he cried, pushing her hands feebly away from him. "My friends... fetch my friends."

"Look, I'm a nurse. Nothing to fear. Someone will call your friends, if you like, but they can't look after you. I can."

"I have their numbers, I'll call," offered Selena. She pulled out her phone and called Jill, while Marisa tried to persuade James to let her examine him.

"We're on our way," the woman's voice said. "Tell the nurse not to handle him."

"But—" Selena began. Jill had already hung up.

"She says not to touch him," Selena said weakly.

Marisa sighed. "Not even first aid? Oh, well. I have to handle all sorts of cases like this at the hospital. The ambulance won't be long. I'll stay here, anyway."

As it happened, James' two friends arrived before the ambulance. They hurried over, dropping their equipment on the ground near him.

"How bad is it?" Jill asked.

"I think the leg is broken," said Marisa, "but he won't let me check."

But, Selena noticed, Jill hadn't been talking to the nurse. James replied in a language Selena didn't recognise, while George took an odd-looking instrument from his pocket and ran it across the leg.

"We can handle this aboard," George said.

Aboard what? Selena wondered.

She soon found out.

Jill turned to her with a smile. "We've paid in advance, haven't we? Tell your mother thanks for a good stay, but we have to go now."

"Now?" cried Marisa. "How? The roads out of town are blocked. And the ambulance is on its way—"

Jill smiled again. "We'll manage. But thank you for your help."

"But what about your stuff?" Selena began. They weren't listening.

The two journalists picked up their equipment and George twisted a knob on his backpack straps. The three of them disappeared in front of Selena, Tom and Tom's two companions, like a film dissolve.

"Strewth!" murmured one of Tom's companions, a middle-aged man called Eric, a reporter for a Melbourne TV station. "No way I can report on *that*." He wiped his forehead.

"I did film it," Tom said, "but I can't see anyone believing it, even if we showed it."

"I'm not sure / believed it," Eric replied honestly. "Probably best to stick to what we came for."

"Well, I'm keeping it for a souvenir," Tom said. "I want to watch it on the couch, back at the B and B."

"Go," agreed Eric. "We've pretty much wrapped for tonight. I'll meet you in the editing suite."

"Come on, Selena... Want to come along, Marisa?"

But Marisa shook her head. "I've had a long shift and I need to collapse on *my* couch!"

That was when the ambulance arrived.

When Selena and Tom arrived at Koala Lodge, she ran up to the family room. Their luggage was gone.

Downstairs, setting up the TV to play back the footage, Tom said, "Well, if they could teleport themselves on to their ship, why not their things? We won't be seeing them again, Selena. Mind you, I have no idea how they can keep a spaceship hidden in this day and age."

"Why did we have aliens here of all places?" wondered Selena. "In the middle of the bushfires?"

"Hey, they were journalists, weren't they? Just not for any publication on our planet."

He pressed play and they saw the scene they'd just watched, from his viewpoint. Again, James groaned, Thando's Mum offered help, the others arrived, they all disappeared. Tom was right. Nobody would believe it.

Tom grinned at her. "Check this one out. They had their own equipment, but the first day here they were using something I lent them before transferring it to their own gadgets, which, I have to say, were like nothing on this earth... They must have forgotten. And I forgot too, I only just watched it before you came back downstairs." He slotted the card into his reader. They watched what must have been the rough footage. It was not in English. And the interviewees were not humans. They were... a couple of koalas. A kangaroo. A wombat.... And they were *answering* questions asked in the language of the aliens.

"But—why here and now? Surely they had their own stories where they came from?"

He shrugged. "Who knows? I'm guessing, from some things they said in the pub, that they don't have much left where they come from, for the same reason that we've been going through this horrendous summer. So they're telling stories from where they visit, to other worlds. Think they'll do any good?"

Selena wondered, too, and remembered that H.G Wells' Martians had invaded when their own planet was in bad shape.

She sighed. "I don't know. In the old days the camera didn't lie. Now..."

"Speaking of lying cameras, I have to go and do some editing." He stood and packed his things. "I'll keep this footage—just in case. See you after dinner!"

Selena looked out at the red sky, after he had left, turning on her laptop for a session on Instagram. The Martians had come and gone, she thought, even if they hadn't wreaked destruction.

H.G Wells would have loved it.

Fires of the Heart

E.E. King

I don't usually do romance, but there was a call for charity stories for the Australian Red Cross—I'm heartsick at the losses so I tried.

It wasn't romantic enough.

I had planned to rewrite it, but when Oz is Burning, an anthology to benefit wild Australia came along, I sent it in.

I was inspired by a Ray Bradbury story where a dead girl emerges from the ocean to finish a sandcastle—the idea of footprints telling a story has stayed with me.

E.E. King

OZ is Burning

Fires of the Heart
by
E.E. King

Chloe pushed back her helmet, wiped her dirty face with an even dirtier rag and sighed.

They were losing. Turned back by winds. Burnt, blackened, charred, and singed. The cries of animals were drowned out by the crackle of brush and fizzing of sap, but she could hear them in her soul.

This was her land, the outback. The vast heartland. The incredible heartache. A place of exquisite beauty and wildness. An expanse of lush abundance and harsh inhospitality. It was quintessentially Australian. She'd grown up here, tagging along with her dad to the old Crow's Nest Fire Station long before it had modernized. She felt connected to every blade of grass and each tree. It was home to all people that she knew and every animal that she loved.

Pans of water set round the edges of the burn, boiled and evaporated, turning to steam faster than any creature could find them.

Two of the six regulars, from her station, Sid and Joe, had been injured. Joe, burned so badly, his right arm was now completely useless. And Sid, poor, sweet Sid who had always seen only the good in everyone and everything, sweet Sid could now see nothing at all.

The rest, experienced combatants all, had been dispersed to buck up other places and train new volunteers.

Twenty of Chloe's new recruits had suffered burns so bad they might never recover. And at least twenty more had been sent to hospital, or home to recover. This, at a time when gusts fanned the flames like bellows, encouraging them to further fury. They needed more firefighters, not fewer, but everyone had been called. Volunteers had seeped out the pores of the poorest towns and the tiniest hamlets.

Heartwarming stories had trickled in from all over the country, old ladies who'd set up care and feeding stations in their yards and nurseries in their bedrooms. Teens who roamed the country, collecting injured animals in their station wagon and nursing them back to a semblance of health. Schools that had turned gymnasiums into tent cities for the myriad of folks whose homes had gone up in flame. Golden Retrievers snuck out for a day of adventuring, that had returned home with orphaned koalas clinging to their backs. She'd be proud of her people and the animals too—if only she weren't so damn sad.

She wiped her eyes one last time, drank down a toxic tasting electrolyte mix and headed back to the bush. She was the only one at the makeshift station. There should have been at least ten. It wasn't safe for her to be alone, no one to call for backup. No one to help with the hoses, no one to pull her out if she got trapped, but safety procedures had gone up in smoke, gone up like the whole god forsaken county.

It was odd to be here alone, or it would have been, if she'd had time to think.

Chloe had been helping fight fires here since she'd been a girl, first with her dad, then with Billie, Sam, Joe, Sid and Vickie. They'd been like a family, sometimes joined by volunteers, but usually just the six of them. Now they'd been separated. They were experienced and each had to go where the need burned fiercest.

For all she knew the others might be dead, dead or burnt beyond recognition. The only ones she knew were "safe", if you could call it that, were the one-armed Joe and sweet, blind Sid. She closed her eyes, picturing them all drunkenly dancing on her last birthday. Her swaying in Billie's arms as she longed for Vickie.

They were the only two women in any of the nearby stations and Chloe had loved Vickie for as long as she had known her.

To Chloe they had seemed a magician's rope. Take two separate pieces, knot them together, slide the knot off, and the rope is whole. She wanted wholeness.

She resented the illogic of the heart. She hated being lost on a path she knew could have no good ending. But feelings were tricky. Even though she knew love was hopeless, emotion, soft as fog, sticky as a spider's web, wrapped around her heart, trapping her, making her feel heavier than stone.

What was the difference between being in love and loving, between a friendship, a friend and a lover? Was it the sex, bodily fluids strong as fate and thicker than blood? Or was it imagining a future stretching ahead, like a land of dreams so various and unknowable?

And how could she tell her mum? Mum, who had suffered so much already, losing her husband to flames, having her only daughter join the force—learning she was gay might kill her.

Chloe shook her head and headed back out. When she reached the blaze, three firefighters stood there, oddly still and silent as if waiting for direction. A fireball rolled toward one. The man ducked and hopped away with an incredible agility. Chloe had never seen anyone react so fast. Was he an acrobat, a gymnast? But there was no time to ask questions, no time to introduce herself, or discuss strategy—no time even to think. Australia was burning.

Side by side they battled the flames, all through the day and all through the night—though there was no more day and night. The land was red and the sky black, broken, not by sun or stars but only by bolts of lightning caused by the heat. Time had stopped. All that was natural, the forward march of season, the transformation of light to night, all had ceased.

The newcomers worked like nothing and no one Chloe had ever seen. They worked for hours without a pause—without talking, without stopping for even a sip of water, or to wipe the soot from their dirty faces. She had only rested a few times, and not for long enough, but she had rested. It was vital.

"Hi," said Chloe. "Time for a break. You two come with me. You two stay here."

She began to walk toward the station. No one followed.

"Come on," she said. "You'll get too exhausted. Burned out—literally." The four turned and looked at her. Their eyes were round and dark, almost without whites in their dirty faces. They stared at her over the filthy kerchiefs wrapped around their noses, seemingly uncomprehending.

Well, she thought, *anyone would be dazed, working as they had.*

"Break," she commanded, again but the four turned back to the fire, fighting as if their lives depended on it. They did.

Chloe turned away, her own eyes watering, not from the heat, but from imagination, and memory. Her own dad had perished in a burn when she was fourteen. Now, for all she knew, everyone she worked with—everyone she loved, might be gone. This land, her land, forest and trees filled with wonderful creatures, wombats, koalas, kangaroos and wallabies had been devastated. Who knew where these strangers had come from? Who knew whom they had lost, or the stories of their heartbreaks?

"Okay," she threw up her hands and turned toward the shack. "I'm going down. Be back in half an hour. Get me if you need me."

She should have protested. She was the one in command, the authority here, but human rack, power and control had burned away. What could she say? That they were endangering themselves? They knew that. That they were endangering others? It was too late for that.

Alone in the shack she wiped off her face and sat down on the couch. Something about those eyes was haunting her. She just meant to have a drink of water, maybe shut her eyes for five minutes, but when she woke up, she knew hours had passed. Why hadn't the alarm gone off? Why hadn't anyone come to get her? Were they alright? Had everyone died?

Outside it was so dark she didn't know if it was day or night. Embers fell around her like burnt moth wings, like the crumbled endings of so many hopes and dreams.

On the borders of the blaze, two more fighters had joined the fray. Where had they come from? Had the fire died out in other places?

"Hello, she shouted. No one turned to her, but whether they couldn't hear her over the crackle of brush and falling trees, or because no one cared, she didn't know. She didn't care. She was going to do her job, damn it. She was going to make them rest, keep them safe, or at least safer. She stepped forward.

A blazing tree swayed and crashed down across her path. It was an old tree that had stood for centuries, weathering countless conflagrations, but this one had been too much.

She backed up; leaves of flames billowed toward her. She jumped backward, turning to run. One of the giant's branches, big enough to be a tree burned through, dropping on the other side of her.

Fire surrounded Chloe leaping and dancing like the ghosts of dying dryads. It was terrifying and eerily beautiful.

So, this is the way my world ends, she thought *Not with a whimper, or a bang, not struggling to save lives in a blaze of glory, or in my lover's arms, but in a sad, useless, sizzle of smoke.*

Why didn't I tell Vickie I loved her? Why wasn't I honest with Billie. I should have lived more and worried less.

Two of the strangers turned and grabbed the fiery tree.

They must have lost all feeling in their hands, she thought. *Even with gloves, how can they...*

Another pulled her to him, hugging her tightly as he raced back to the shack. Through the rubber clothing he felt oddly soft. Had they been issued some new type of padding that she wasn't familiar with? She stared into the eyes, so big, so brown, so round. They grew into a total darkness that engulfed the shack, the sky and the earth.

***

Chloe woke up in the hospital, her hands and head so tightly bound she couldn't move. Clean straight lines of gauze framed her vision.

How odd, she thought, *now I am encased by white, before everything was red and black.* She longed for the new green of trees, the cobalt skies and the deep, deep indigo of Vickie's eyes. Chloe marveled at this yearning, thicker than fog, stronger than oceans, hotter than fire.

And then—Vickie's beautiful face bent over her.

"Chloe," she said, tears fattened by joy streamed down her face like welcoming rain.

"I thought I'd lost you."

She took Chloe's bandaged hand between her own, squeezing it so tightly Chloe gasped. The intake of breath made Chloe's ribs ache.

"Sorry," Vickie said laughing and sobbing a little at the same time. "It's just that I thought I'd never see you again... never get to tell you how I felt.

"You were all alone at the station, working solo for days. When they found you in the shack you were delirious."

"What?" said Chloe.

"Wait." Her voice felt rough and unused. Each word burned.

"How long was I out?" she whispered.

"A month," Vickie said.

A month of darkness. Not the darkness of smoke and embers but the deeper night of the unconscious.

"The fires?"

"Out," Vickie said. "Finally, out."

"But I wasn't alone," Chloe said. "There were these firefighters who joined me—fearless, tireless with round, dark eyes and..."

"Hush now," said Vickie. Hush, my love. You need to sleep and heal. When one is wounded the mind sees things it needs to see.

***

It was another month before she was well enough to go home. Home to the new cottage she and Vickie had rented.

She was so grateful. Grateful for her life. Grateful for her Vickie. Grateful that her mother was safe and had been so glad to have Chloe back, she didn't care whom Chloe chose to love. But her joy cast shadows of loss and sorrow. How could she be happy when so much was lost?

***

Chloe was running over a meadow of smoldering coals. Her soles were burning. She could smell, but not feel them. Flames raged around her, stroking her arms, singeing her skin. Her flesh blackened and crumbled falling into the earth, crumbling into ash. But still she ran. Legs of bone, racing over fields of glowing embers. Beside her, animals were fleeing too, wombats, koalas, kangaroos and wallabies, their fur aflame, their large, round, dark eyes empty.

"Shhh, shhh, my sweet. You're safe. It's over now." Vickie's arms encased her.

Chloe flinched at the touch, terrified that her skin might crack. Fearful of the white bone underneath.

Then she clung to Vickie, a solid thing in a sea of mist and nightmare.

"Was it the dream again?" Vickie whispered, stroking her hair.

**

Slowly, slowly like young growth sprouting from charred earth, reports began to come in from the front lines of the battle that had at long last been won. First, they were just a trickle, then a stream, then a torrent—accounts of unexpected, round-eyed firefighters that appeared from nowhere. Firefighters who worked wordlessly, jumping, leaping and sometimes almost flying over the flames with inhuman agility. Warriors who toiled without pausing for food, or water.

**

Two months later when Chloe was finally strong enough, she wandered out to the charred fields, leaning on Vickie's arm.

There among the ashes like hollow men, were six empty uniforms, each stained by the prints of the muddy paws of wombats, koalas, kangaroos and wallabies. Chloe knelt beside them, and like the tracker she was, saw each muddy print coming in from the burn, going back out to the blackened land, and never returning.

OZ is Burning

Pay Back

Alex Isle

As climate changes in Australia, how will it change us? Would we shed an entire region of a country, fast becoming unlivable, to save the rest? What happens to people who don't want to leave it? I came to write this story while thinking about how that might begin.

Alex Isle

Pay Back
by
Alex Isle

Jonas and his mule smelled smoke, but the fire was mercifully distant. They moved at an identical slow pace, wasting no energy that might be held back from the relentless sun. Jonas wondered whether they should have waited for night. Probably if they had, the wind would have changed and sent that fire hurtling at them. With so few remaining to fight them, many fires did as they pleased, and humans had no choice but to retreat from their lands.

"Don't even think about it," he said aloud, smacking back a grey muzzle with the back of a practised hand. The muzzle withdrew, just as though his mule, Mary Jane, hadn't considered a quick snack of human to bring some fun to her day. They got on well as a rule, about as well as a human and a mule ever could, but you couldn't ignore mule nature.

Two days had brought him west from his country town to the outskirts of the failing city. There were vague shadows ahead suggesting buildings and Jonas picked up the pace. Mary Jane wheezed and resisted, but finally shook her head and followed. She was fairly fresh; they had found a remote house in which to rest overnight and it was still early morning.

The doctor wasn't looking forward to seeing the city he'd left so many years before. His two tours of duty in Afghanistan had not left him with any illusions about human charity. Everyone was out for themselves. Those without those instincts generally didn't make it these days, if they weren't in some nation that made a virtue of looking after the helpless. As the climate became ever more inhospitable, the city shrank.

"C'mon," Jonas said to Mary Jane, rearranging the packs on her back to make room. "Last few klicks, you can carry me. We'll get to the food faster, I promise."

He rode down the centre of St Georges Terrace, the mule's hooves sending echoes down that canyon of glass and concrete. Wind blew around them, but Jonas heard no voices, and the few vehicles veered around them, their drivers not even bothering to curse him. The temperature was rising fast, though it couldn't be much beyond seven am or so. The feel of the place, Jonas thought, was of somewhere that had given up.

He nudged the mule's sides, urging her into a more energetic stride as they turned into Victoria Terrace, the area long dominated by the Catholic Church, whose offices, a walled convent and a school, surrounded the old cathedral. Once that building would have towered over everything else. In this secular age, it too was overshadowed by the hulking faded-red brick hospital just past its wrought iron gates.

Here there were so many buses and vans and other large vehicles out front of the hospital that Jonas slid down from the saddle again. He watched ambulatory and chairbound patients being escorted out to them and wondered, for these weren't ambulances or patient transports. "You closing down the hospital?" he asked the nearest paramedic, loading an old man in his manual wheelchair up the ramp of a Wine Tours bus.

The guy looked distractedly at him as though wondering where he'd sprung from. "They moved up the Evac," he said. "I think it's still stage three, though. Are you looking for a patient?"

"Dr. Christina Chang. She asked me to meet her here."

"Inquiries is through there." With that the paramedic dismissed him and kept on with his work. Jonas led Mary Jane to the doors and hesitated, not wanting to leave her here, where there could be threats not so easily dealt with by an accurate hoof to the guts. Then he shrugged slightly and carried on in, heading straight over to the bulletproof glass Information window.

"That's a donkey," said the woman behind it.

"Mule," Jonas said agreeably. "I'm looking for Dr. Christina Chang."

"Computers are down, so I can't look anything up," the woman said. "They have been since Wednesday and since we're at stage three, they might not bother to reconnect us. Do you know what department she's in?"

Jonas was about to answer "Psych" when he heard a certain voice behind him. He turned quickly, and saw the back of a woman with shiny black hair, patiently persuading a very large man, clutching a teddy bear, along the hallway.

"Now will you take a bus ride?" she asked him in the tone of one in the last five per cent of her patience. "We found Joey! You and Joey can both take a bus ride, okay?"

"Will I get my meds? Hey, donkey!"

"Jonas, I hope that's you." She glanced back quickly, still speaking to her anxious patient. "The nurse on the bus will give you your meds. Now come on, please!" She quickly hugged Jonas before dodging a snap from Mary Jane. "I'd given up on you! It's been weeks."

"I only got your message five days ago and I started in as soon as I could."

"Weren't you at your practice? I talked to Malcolm on the radio."

"I was on the road. Didn't he tell you that?"

"I don't know, too much static." She waved it off, impatiently. "Harry, I want you to head outside to the buses. Jonas, get him out there, would you? I'll join you in a few minutes."

A few turned out to be perhaps half an hour before the weary Christina made it outside to where Jonas and Mary Jane had taken refuge beneath the scant shade of an awning. Jonas noted with some surprise that she was being followed by a boy of about thirteen or fourteen in plain black T-shirt and shorts, an ancient paperback book in his hand. Another patient? Christina drank water from an already-warm bottle and offered it to Jonas, who took it with a nod of thanks, took a swig and held it towards the boy, who quickly shook his head.

"How's Malcolm?" Christina asked.

"He's good. Still kind of a fish out of water, but he's pretty well taken over at the courthouse since no judges come to us on circuit anymore and the last cop was moved out two years ago."

Christina Chang smiled. "You must have met him on pretty much the last case that Winston ever had with lawyers and judge from out of town."

"Yeah, I think so. But enough on my love life. So, what's happening? You know you don't need to make a thing out of asking me for help. Anything for you, Chrissie."

She laughed. "Not *anything*. What you promised my dad. Just that." More quietly she said, "The kid behind me is named Ali. He was admitted for gastro a couple of weeks ago, but I've been keeping him in the hospital because he's got nowhere to go. No family that he'll admit to, and he's headed for the worst of the camps..."

"What camps? He an illegal?"

Chang sighed deeply. "Does that really matter now? Where do you think most of the people without family are going when they get to Sydney or Melbourne or wherever, Jonas? I'll give you a clue; it's not the Marriott Hotel. Unaccompanied teenaged boys over thirteen are going to a single men's work camp. This kid won't last a week."

"And you're telling me this sad story because?"

"You're not planning to head over the border, are you, Jonas."

He shook his head, half negative, half pure confusion. "Why the fuck would I do that? I don't need this city anyway. I only came in because I promised you I would, Chrissie. Stupid dumb promise anyway; where the hell was my brain?"

She grinned suddenly, but her face returned to sad in a moment.

"Half pickled, if my dad's to be believed. 'I forgot to get my goddaughter a gift when she was born and moral guidance went out the window, but any time she needs help, I promise, she can ask me. But only for a big thing. Any piddly little problem, she's got to ask you' "–that's what my dad said you told him. So here's my big thing, Jonas. Take on Ali as an apprentice."

"Chris–it's not the eighteenth century and even then, you had to go to freaking medical school."

"Whatever you want to call it."

"Anyway, does the kid even want to be a doctor?"

"Ask him."

"Chrissie!" Jonas sighed and took a step towards the kid. "Hi, Ali," he said, as though meeting the kid in his surgery back home. He glanced at the book. Actual paper books were oddities, but he supposed if they had a holdout anywhere, it'd be in a hospital or anywhere else with no entertainment budget. *Old Man's War*, the title said.

"That's a new one on me," Jonas said, nodding towards it. "I'm an old man and they've got no use for me in any war these days. Been to enough war already." Ali was looking at him again, evidently he was now interesting enough to warrant some attention, Jonas thought with amusement. "Okay, Ali," he said. "I'm Jonas, friend of your doc here, and she's asked me to talk to you. You know what's going on here with the hospital?"

"It's the third stage of the evacuation," Ali said, matter of fact. "They're moving all patients able to be safely transported." He put down the book on the table. "Not that there are all that many. They've been moving the more serious cases one at a time over months."

"You want to go live in Melbourne or wherever?"

"No."

"What job do you think you can do here if the infrastructure is completely broken up?"

"I dunno."

He didn't seem too worried, Jonas thought. That or he couldn't conceive of Jonas's suggestion actually coming true.

"Dr Chang thinks I should take you on as an apprentice, turn you into a doctor, 18th century style. What do you think of that? And a clue, the answer is not, ' "I dunno." '

The kid had some smarts, Jonas thought, seeing the boy think over what he'd said, staring at Mary Jane while he did so. He was skinny–and Chris had said he'd had gastro–but overall he seemed to be in decent shape.

"I can learn stuff," he said after a few moments. "I learned English when I was ten. Came over here on a boat; stuck on

41

one of those offshore places they don't tell you folks about anymore."

"Maybe not, but I know about them," Jonas said. "Did your parents come with you?"

Ali's face went tight, suddenly much more adult and he shook his head, finally. Jonas could push, but he sensed if he did, Ali would end the conversation. "Okay," he said wearily. "You can tag along back to my town and we'll see how good you are at learning stuff. For now, we're going to camp out under one of those half-dead street trees while I get some rest."

Someone had come up to Christina and she was already heading away with him. Ali followed in Jonas' wake. Presently they watched another bus drive into the pick up area and nurses began to shepherd people aboard. Christina cut loose from them and hurried over to Jonas and Ali.

"An update," she told them. "We just got the word that everyone needs to be out of this place by this evening."

"What's the rush?"

"I don't exactly know."

"What about you?"

She gestured behind her. "I'll be escorting this busload."

Jonas got to his feet, rubbing his shoulder, and assessed the situation. He frowned a little as he studied her. "Why the fuck don't they organise flights? They're not out of fuel supplies yet and I know they're still running fly in/fly outs to mine sites. They're going to kill some of these patients, even if they're not terminal at the moment, by jolting them all the way to Adelaide and beyond on those buses."

"It's not my decision," Chang said wearily. "It's politics. Look, I didn't get much sleep for the last few nights and I've got to go help out again. Ali can show you where to get something to eat."

She hurried off, leaving them to look warily at one another. Jonas told the kid they would be heading back out of the city once he and Mary Jane had had a night's rest. "She's a bit stiff in the left hind," he explained. "Comes from an injury a few years ago, so I have to be careful if she's done a long walk."

"You didn't ride her all the way, did you?" Ali accused.

"Come on, kid, do I look like someone who mistreats an animal? No. Only the last stretch. You'll be carrying as much as she does, trust me."

"Great," said Ali.

Jonas made his decision then. "Look, I've changed my mind about overnighting here. Where's this place we can get some food? We'll rest–don't get me wrong–but out of the city."

"What about Dr Chang?"

Jonas sighed, not able to see Christina anywhere around now. It felt bad to just go without saying goodbye to her, but she had said she would be accompanying one of the busloads. "She's busy. If we see her, we'll say goodbye, but I don't feel comfortable around here. You?"

Ali shook his head. "We want to go past Emergency and down the hill, around to the other side of the hospital," he said.

As their little procession passed the wrought iron gates of the cathedral, Jonas saw a young priest standing there, looking uncomfortable in the trad black gown and tight, white dog collar. She stood out because of that and also her stillness.

She stared at him, everyone did, thanks to the damn mule. He was aware of her scrutiny, which was curious but perfectly polite, but Jonas knew what he looked like; a scruffy old man with longish hair, mostly grey, with a few determined strands of brown hanging on and gingery tints in his swagman's-style beard. His clothes were comparatively clean and in good repair; a doctor couldn't afford to look like a derelict, but they were the same basic clothes a farmer would have worn. Probably, he looked like he was older than his seventy two years. The sun did that to a guy; both in Afghanistan and now here, increasingly merciless. Afghanistan made him think of Ali. *I'll have to get Ali a hat; he's not wearing one. Damn you, Christina, why couldn't you have asked me for a kidney instead of giving me a kid?*

Everybody else around the priest, in the hospital drop off point and on the pavements, was dashing about like idiots. The city was still too full of idiots, Jonas thought. Loud honking made them scatter, but slowly, as a shiny black and official looking car slid into their midst. A group of soldiers followed the car and surrounded it, bodyguard-style. The driver of the nearest bus, who had driven forward a few metres, braked hard. Jonas could see him gesticulating angrily from his seat. He hurried forward as best he could and tapped the arm of the nearest person. "What's going on, do you know?"

"They're tryin' to make my auntie leave." This was a muscular Aboriginal guy in his twenties, Jonas guessed, scrappily dressed in khaki shorts and an ancient t-shirt. He presented his problem to Jonas as simply as a child.

"Was she a patient in the hospital?"

"Yeah, she was there for dialysis, but she doesn't stay in, she just has the treatment and comes home, you know? They can't make her go anywhere!"

"What about the fuckhead in the shiny car?"

"He come in with the army trucks behind, they're there," a girl called nearby. Jonas looked, seeing the trucks parked under the huge Moreton Bay fig tree which had dominated Murray Street leading up to the cathedral for decades. In its deep shade, they were about as inconspicuous as such vehicles could get.

"Right. Excuse me," Jonas said politely to those around him and began to push his way through the throng until he was at the car, with two people in khaki blocking his access to the car's rear window. He waved at the man sitting inside and began to speak, introducing himself and describing his journey until curiosity did the job and the automatic window slid down.

"Who the hell are you?" a male voice asked.

"Dr Wallace. And you?"

"My name is Price. I'm the Minister for Emergency Services, here to speak to your colleagues..."

Jonas didn't bother to correct his assumption. "Well, I'm just here to give you a small piece of advice, Minister."

"What would that be?"

"A lot of these people are here to collect one lady on that bus. If she's allowed to disembark, this situation is going to ease down a few notches. Then if you move this car out of the way and take your soldier boys and girls with you, it'll calm down even more."

"Dr Wallace, I don't think you understand the situation. I've been tasked by the Federal Government to oversee the evacuation of this hospital to facilities in Adelaide. We're moving to stage 4 now because of–well, events have been shifted back and so you need to get off this road. Help him out of the area, please."

Abruptly Jonas was the focus of several of the soldiers, who closed firmly around him, a couple of them reaching for his arms. He freed himself with two simple, downwards jerks of his wrists and stepped quickly clear. "Go get your auntie, mate," he shouted to the man who had spoken to him and the guy nodded eagerly, calling to the people around him. They surged towards the bus, drumming fists on its door and making such a racket that the driver swore–Jonas could see him outline the word–and opened it up.

"Everybody wait," the big guy yelled out and went aboard on his own. Jonas nodded, giving due credit for brains. All of them getting on would have created panic among the bus passengers. In moments the guy was backing off the bus, escorting a small dark-skinned elderly woman with bushy white hair, who moved with a wobbly dignity. Her relatives nearly knocked her over with their greeting and swiftly whisked her away. Behind her, a half dozen others clambered off the bus, some calling out to people. The others seemed content to stay on or perhaps were too ill to care, Jonas thought grimly.

"Out of the way!" he called out, using his memory of the military to project his voice. "Let the bus go!"

When it was on its way, Jonas looked for Ali and Mary Jane and found them past the iron gates, on the cathedral grounds. Mary Jane had her head down in the surviving nasturtiums and Ali was apparently in a serious conversation with the priest.

Seeing Jonas, Ali waved energetically. "Yeah, yeah, give me a minute," the doctor grumbled.

"No, Dr Jonas, look behind you!"

He did, seeing the suited Minister out of his car, the soldiers around him. The politician pointed to Jonas, his face tight with anger, and the soldiers moved forward towards him. Jonas understood only too well: The others in the crowd were gone and out of his reach. Jonas was the only one left whom he could punish.

The young priest blocked the way of the soldiers and shook her head firmly at the uniformed woman. "I'm sorry, you can't come in."

"That man's under arrest…"

"You aren't police so you can't arrest him," the priest pointed out, "and he's on church land so he has sanctuary."

"Come on, there is no sanctuary anymore!"

"There is if I say so," the priest responded.

"Get a police officer!" the soldier called back to her comrades.

The priest returned quickly to Jonas and Ali. "Get moving while they figure it out."

"Figure what out?" Jonas asked. "That they're a mob of morons."

"No, the Minister there is the moron," the priest corrected. "I'll do penance for saying that, but it's worth it. Also, for lying by implication. The soldier was correct; sanctuary hasn't been a thing for a long time. But there's no call to arrest you. It's just a matter of face saving."

Jonas looked back over at the scene of frantic medical professionals and patients being organised onto the final bus. Sweat was pouring off him and he was mildly surprised not to have noticed this, or his need for about a litre of cold water. "Are you going to be okay?" he asked reluctantly, not at all sure what he'd do if the priest said no.

"Not sure," the priest said, her grey eyes calm as she studied him. "It's strange days."

"You've got that right."

Still uncertain, Jonas nodded and turned to make his not-so-speedy getaway. He walked along beside the mule, Ali on her other side, up the circular driveway that led to the cathedral building, then at the boy's direction, left to go through the aboveground carpark reserved for cathedral staff and workers. No cars there now. Down past empty flowerbeds to a second set of iron gates, standing open.

Jonas' pace was already slow and he sighed at the thought of the sixteen kilometres to Midland under the sun, where he knew there was a camp that would let them rest awhile–and treat a few folks-before the longer, more difficult journey back home. So why had he stopped before those gates, his hand on the mule's bridle.

"Oh, fuck it."

"Hey!" Ali said reprovingly. "You're in a fucking house of God, man."

"Church is over there. I'm outside," Jonas muttered at him. He thought of all those people milling around with no blasted idea. "Come on. Let's get those supplies and–and then once this mob are out of the way, we can gather these folks together."

"I knew Dr Chang wouldn't pass me over to someone who'd ignore folks in need," Ali said solemnly.

"Kids as smart arsed as you don't generally live long, you know that?"

"Better hurry it up, old man."

As they went, Jonas heard shouts and engine noise, moving away from them. Very fast. He glanced at Ali and they shrugged at one another.

***

Jonas wasn't surprised, somehow, to find maybe twenty, thirty people waiting in the lobby, surrounding, god help him, Auntie in a wheelchair with a bright crotched cover over her bony knees and her family protectively around her. But he hadn't expected to see Christina Chang standing next to the young priest.

"There's some sort of riot going on downtown," Chang said. "Apparently the Parliament is being looted."

"Where the fuck are the politicians?"

"Being evacuated. That's apparently what they used the last planes for. The Emergency Minister came to invite our chief surgeon and his family aboard. And stop swearing."

"The last…" Jonas decided it was time to stop pretending to be, excuse him, the straight man. "So what the–why the hurry up?"

"Something's going to happen in the city, something to do with them making everyone get out of the CBD. I was on a bus with some of these people, but we ran into a mob and couldn't go any further."

"You going to tell me, or do I have to go on echoing you like a retarded parrot?"

"There's a bomb," called out someone. Auntie's nephew, raising his hand like a kid desperate to tell teacher the answer. An alarmed series of squawks and comments went through the assembled group and Auntie tugged at the big guy's other hand until he leaned down. She smacked his head and hissed something in his ear.

"Sorry, auntie!"

"What bomb?" Jonas asked, resigning himself to his role.

"We don't know," Christina Chang said, speaking over the whispers and cries. "A member of Auntie's family heard something and told someone who told someone who eventually got back here and told me. We don't have proof, we don't know anything, but five minutes ago every cop and soldier disappeared. And the refugees started gathering in here. I had no idea why until you showed up. I thought you'd be halfway out of the city by now."

"Working on it," Jonas grumbled. "So somebody wants to blow up Parliament? Not very bloody original."

Auntie studied him keenly and nodded as though she was conducting a job interview and thought he had potential. She said something to her nephew, who ushered the young priest closer to Auntie's chair."

"Ah, she says we need to follow the man with the mule."

***

They made it between five and ten kilometres eastwards out of the city, reaching the first deserted ring of suburbia, before the earth shuddered faintly under their feet. They stopped on the empty highway and turned, milling in indecision, unable to see what had happened in their wake.

The priest came to Jonas' side a few moments later, her white collar showing clearly although she was now wearing lighter, "civilian" clothes rather than the robe.

Why would even a stupid government bomb their own city? Was it poisoning the well before you ran away? Because he feared that was exactly what it was, he closed his eyes for a few moments. He wanted so much just to take Mary Jane and head away from these people, back home to Malcolm and what peace he could get.

"Auntie's sending some people to get us more water and she wants your mule along to carry it back for everyone. Then she needs to talk to you."

"What for? I don't know anything. Also look around, the bush is as dry as a bunch of bones. There's no water out here!"

The priest shrugged. "Auntie seems to think there is. She's given quite detailed directions. You going to argue?"

Jonas sighed deeply and resigned himself. "No, ma'am. Sister. Ah–what is your name?"

"Olivia."

"I guess it's nice to meetcha, Olivia."

They dug for the water, creating a small, muddy, precious well in the midst of dryness, beneath a grove of trees taller and more luxuriant than most of the surrounding forest. Back on the roadside beneath the scant shelter of an abandoned service station, the exhausted people–and one equine-rested and drank and Jonas quietly knelt by Auntie's chair to examine her.

A young woman beside Auntie spoke to her, in what Jonas assumed was the local Nyungar language. Auntie shook her head and answered with a warning tone and the young woman stepped away. Jonas gently took the elder's wrist to test the pulse and did his best to hide concern at the uneven faintness of it.

"We'll get you back to the hospital soon," he assured her. "Whatever idiots set off that bomb are gone now, and we can make you much more comfortable than we can out here, well, some comfortable."

She waved that off with a scornful sort of snort, seeming amused by the suggestion. "I'm goin' back to my country tonight. Too far to get there on my feet, but that's not gonna matter after I go. You got to take everybody and get moving. I told Jared, my nephew. They'll go with you."

"I'm not Moses, Auntie...."

"I'm Stolen Generation. You know what that is? Got put in one of those places with lots of kids from my country and other places, to grow us up white. They wouldn't let our parents see us."

"Same," Jonas said wryly and she blinked curiously at him. "Child of unmarried mother here. They took those babies away then too, gave us to properly married people."

Auntie made a "huh!" sound at that, which he thought pretty well summed up the whole stupid matter.

"Get moving," she said again. "Take 'em out, away from the city. The city's going to break into pieces, and it'll fall. Then this country will heal and those of you that stay can come back. A few staying is okay. You're the ones who can learn. But you can't go back to the city right now."

Deathbed prophet? Jonas wondered, feeling a sudden chill. This elderly woman didn't look near death, though of course she was, within a week if they could not get her continuing dialysis. Elderly? She was probably only his age. The 21st century doctor part of him wanted to hurry her back to the city, to those lifesaving machines probably/possibly still in hospitals. He lifted his head then, smelling smoke drifting on the wind. That fire which had chased him into the city, or another one, burning like an actual sentient creature seeking prey.

"You see?" she asked.

Did he?

Don't read in more than your senses tell you. That bomb, if it was a bomb and rumour didn't dress up an accident or the results of neglect, that scared all of us. We're worried there'll be more if we go back too soon. Easy enough to dream up something supernatural in the words of a dying woman. Easy enough to believe going east to the other cities is somehow going to save us long term. We always want to believe.

"I don't know, Auntie."

"Take these folks somewhere safe. Pay back. You did it, you mend it."

She closed her eyes and for a moment he was afraid she'd die on him then and there–great advertising for a doctor–but then her hand tightened on his and she straightened, sitting like a queen in her wheelchair, there in the dark under the trees, somehow alone in the tight crush of some thirty scared people. And Jonas knew for sure that he wasn't the leader here.

"That fire's not here for us, man. You going to take them?"

"Yes, auntie."

By the Grace of God

Harold Gross

I will never forget seeing the burned out towns along the Great Ocean Road the first time I drove down that amazing stretch many years back. The stark remains of blackened gum trees gave me the barest sense of the intensity and ferocity of the fires that had passed through. When the flames returned in such force and scope this year, I wanted to provide some relief to those who were affected by it all, as well as some ironic questioning as to the ways of the world. My typical response to tragedy is humor; it doesn't fix anything, but it makes it easier to function. Or at least I hope it does.

Harold Gross

OZ is Burning

By the Grace of God
by
Harold Gross

"Oh, crap."

***

That was how it started. The moment.

I realized my mistake nanoseconds before it all unfolded, dividing those moments into picoseconds and then attoseconds as I watched in fascinated horror. I could have stretched that horror out infinitely, but not run it back...eventually, I'd have to just let it occur and move on. Existence is about moving forward, right? So, everything in my considerable existence is now marked as before "oh, crap" and after "oh, crap."

And, before you ask, no I couldn't just jump back and change things. Sure the whole "time's arrow" thing was meaningless then, but even your own species can create self-deleting code which, once launched, just happens. This "oh, crap" moment was stretched across several dimensions. Once begun it was inevitable.

So, I relaxed and allowed the inexorable to unfold.

You should do the same, this could take a while. Take a load off and lean back here in the shade. This really is a magnificent tree. Take in the view while we chat. The fire is still a ways off. But my story, I was telling you my story.

I have to admit it was pretty spectacular: the inexorable, the inevitable. I might have even enjoyed it more if it hadn't been so damned painful.

But I suppose that's what you get when you just screw around with things without thinking them through.

***

Perhaps I should wind this story back a bit and explain. Stories are easier to wind back than time.

55

I like to tinker. I just do. It's fun. And with all of infinity laid out before you, you have to do something to entertain yourself.

I see the same thing in many beings, especially human children, who like to do nothing more than rip things apart and put them back together in unexpected configurations. If you think the platypus and other oddities came about any differently, you're kidding yourself. I should know.

I'm not saying it wasn't evolution... nor was it, how do you refer to it... Intelligent Design? That label just makes me smile and gives me way more credit than due. How about: Lame-Ass Guesses. I pushed things and let them run... just to see what came out the other side after a few millennia... it was often such a gift.

As I said, I like to tinker. So there I was one "day"...

(Remember, time as you would recognize it didn't exist yet... things were just a jumble—all times, all places, all dimensions, all at once. I know it hurts your head to consider this, but just nod and let's move on... for this tale it didn't stay that way very long anyway...)

So, there I was one day with these notions, I would call it a concept, but that would imply a considered decision. It wasn't. I wanted to see what would happen if I mixed them with some ideas and potentials, understanding that the emergent process could get a bit tricky...

This isn't working at all, is it?

OK, let me give you a quick cut from your perspective.

Nothing.

bang

Everything.

***

Here is where it might get a tad confusing, so settle in and put that marinated meat back in the esky till we're done.

Time suddenly existed and I was both at the beginning of it all and falling into some *time* later. As I fell into the well, this pit, that you call Earth, a red haze from the flaming plasma formed around me. The part that was falling wasn't all of me, but it was rather an aspect, a piece of me. My perception was split and remained attached to both *it* in its timeframe and my other *it* in a much earlier timeframe throughout the fall.

There was no opportunity to scream, only feel, even if from some incredible distance. It wasn't a long fall; by my standards it was barely a blip, but it was intense. As the ground rushed up, friction finally slowed me to sub-sonic speeds and the plasma dissipated. A white covered forest spread below me. I could see the animals, feel the life, appreciate the bite of the crisp air rushing past me.

And then I hit and the connection was severed; I felt a tearing. My entire physical presence suddenly refocused to that time and place. I was standing on the edge of a hot dirt berm that stretched out away from me in an arc on both sides; two arms reaching and connecting far on the other side of the impacted ground.

The crater was already filling with water, the earth attempting to make a lake from an injury. The flattened landscape and toppled trees looked like a giant butterfly had fallen on top of the forest. Another beautiful forest lost to fiery disaster, now that I think of it. And in the distance flying away was that other piece of me, quickly shrinking as it approached the horizon, and somehow managing to elude my attempts to follow it.

I guess that's always the way of self-therapy though: the harder you look at yourself, the less you see for a while.

***

Trust me, the event didn't go unnoticed. Really. I can prove it...it made quite the impact.

I hit on the 30th of June, 1908. Sound familiar? Oh, wait, that was the 17th of June according to the calendars where it happened. Seriously, I have never understood how all of you living on the same planet could have different ways of measuring time. So confusing! Well, one of those dates should sound familiar anyway.

Or perhaps the name would be more familiar: The Tunguska Event? I always fancied myself an "event" kind of omniscient being, but all I had to do was show up for this one. No effort required on my part. No choice, either. And this was the first time I'd ever lost any part of myself... it simply wasn't possible before because everything was me. I know that sounds rather self-centered, but this is a literal description, not an analogy.

***

Now, I was functional during the scope of time in between "oh, crap" and this event, though not quite myself as you can imagine. Or not quite all myself? But I was around and doing what I do best, or most anyway: I tinkered. There were galaxies and stars and black holes and some neat oddities to keep all entities guessing, 'cause why not? And, certainly, when I had the chance, I had some fun with anything that was intelligent enough to notice me. I made deals, enforced contracts, and I answered prayers. Yeah, I really did, though certainly not all. Sometimes I made sure there was enough strife to make my arrival and help noticed, and sometimes I just created disaster to see what would happen (remember: tinkerer). There was no great plan, rhyme, or reason. Despite the various texts in the universe, from tablets to odiferous to digital, that attempted to sum it all up, none were even close. A few, however, were entertaining. Old man? Beard? Really? Just how narrow is your thinking?

But Earth had always been a particular point of interest. It took me a long time to understand what my fascination with this particular planet and species was... frankly the dinosaurs and insects were more interesting to look at and lasted a lot longer. It isn't as if you're alone in the universe nor that I haven't been elsewhere. Heck, I'm elsewhere right now... I'm still semi-omniscient (if that concept is even possible. I mean seriously, what is *semi*-omniscient?). And, while I limited you all to that silly sub-light movement, I can bounce around pretty much at will instantaneously.

But back on point, it was the moment of impact that clarified the constant draw for me. Billions of years and I'd had no idea what was going on, why I kept coming back here, but when I felt that moment and that essence arrive, there was clarity. There was a tugging, a resonance that began. It was warm and wonderful and suddenly I realized I'd been cold for eons.

For a moment I was whole again before being sundered. But after that piece flew off, the core of me froze over again.

It was astonishing, which alone was a gift of sorts, but not one I wanted to keep forever. So off I went trying to find it.

***

And here it is, nestled in amongst the Gondwana beeches that grew up around my beneficent essence before the continents cracked and the south froze; a throwback to your planet's nascent days, and a unique example of flora. It has taken quite some time to find this beauty. You'd think the name might have been a hint to me. (Are you sure Gondwana isn't just a mispronunciation of God wanna?) But, it wasn't like it was initially anchored in time any more than I am. Admittedly, only having one planet to search (versus an entire universe) is quite a reduction in variables, assuming, as we now can see, it eventually set down roots and waited. Who knew it would stay in place even in the face of disaster; I guess I/it just wasn't ready.

So, here we are. Quite literally by the grace of god in the shade. Well, shaded by the clouds of smoke and warmed by the lick of distant flame. That whiff of smoking bones is particularly piquant, don't you think? I can tell you do, sitting there with your beer and chunks of charcoal hoping for a nice bit of BBQ while watching the park with so much reality show salivation.

Now I hope I've made it clear that I care not a whit for you, your family, or even your species, but I do care for this tree. It houses the rest of me. I may be eternal, but I don't know if what's in there, separated from me for so long, maintained that benefit. It's a piece I'm not sure I miss yet, but its absence feels like an empty hollow deep within me. It echoes. It's like having one-half of a conversation with myself when I plan something. I'm always right either way, but it just feels like an unsupported chord. Unfinished.

How can I explain this in a way you'll understand?

Here is what I think I do know: In this tree is what is good in me, almost in its entirety. Understand? It lives here within, part of its fiber, part of its bark and sap. (Ooh, I like how that came out... would you mind writing that one down for later. I'm sure this will end up as a parable or something at some point. Heck, you can even write it.)

What it comes down to is that I don't know how to stitch it back into myself quite yet. But I've got plenty of time to figure that out, well about a millennium anyway if we treat it well. See, seems like now that I'm so close to it, I don't want to go anywhere or anywhen on a whim as I did before. This tree is going to be my hobby for a while. At least until I succeed. Or it dies.

But I see no reason to hasten that event, despite those columns of smoke in the valley. If you look, you can even see flames dancing on the distant canopy.

Basically, I could use some help. So, what I'm asking is for you to get up off your arse, put down that bloody lager, and walk away from your plans for this knoll and the firepit you dug way too close to its delicate bark for my comfort, and within sight of a greater conflagration (which is just obscene).

Consider what my tree has survived and switch to smoothies or something while we create a firebreak and give me the time I need to figure this all out.

I can make it worth your while, you know, if you're willing to make a deal. What do you desire more than anything? I've a contract right here we can sign, if you're ready and then we can really dig in.

Should Fire Remember the Fuel?

Kyla Lee Ward

Dreams of home, family, and safety keep first responders anchored and sane. It allows ordinary people to perform heroic feats and keep going in the face of exhaustion and pain. But those dreams are as fragile as the scarred landscape. I bought this story because I ache for those who lost so much while serving the greater good.

Phyllis Irene Radford

OZ is Burning

Should Fire Remember the Fuel?
by
Kyla Lee Ward

A little past sixteen hundred hours, the wind changed, and Mark saw it happen. He saw old Alfie Pozzoli burn.

Alfie was on the dozer, reinforcing the existing fire break between the bush reserve and the paddocks surrounding Fairlie town. He'd gouged a fresh, brown scar across the mouth of the shallow valley that was the fire's potential approach. A bad day at the end of a bad Summer: the grass here was like yellowed paper and the wind like standing in front of an open kiln.

Mark trudged up the western slope into the wind with a drip torch dribbling fire from his hand: he waved it in long, slow arcs, controlling the back burn. In his wake lay metres of charred ground, and Rory was performing the same back-breaking dance to his right. He felt his own sweat pooling inside his gloves. He and all the other members of the striker team wore full kit with filter masks and goggles, for there was smoke in the air, even though at last report the fire was still forty or more kilometres to the north.

The fire had kindled early this morning, right in the heart of the reserve. While the wind was blowing west to east, the danger to the town itself was low, but reinforcing the break was an obvious precaution. The striker was the smallest of any of the tankers, but it was all that could be spared. The bulk of the Fairlie branch of the Rural Fire Service (together with a unit sent from the regional headquarters), were north and east on the highway. That was where the main fire threatened the meatworks and historic vineyard—and that, as Alfie had said, was that and a prayer.

Rory was a ginger giant, his skin one huge freckle, and the owner of the Fairlie petrol station and garage. Beside him, Mark felt short and obscurely pale. Through the spitting and popping of their torches, Mark heard him mutter, "The heat, they say: so fires light themselves now?" He glanced at Mark through his goggles. "You mark my words, this'll all turn out to be a couple of bloody kids!"

Go ahead and ask me, Mark thought. He taught years seven through ten, after all. If Rory truly believed this was the work of children, he should ask him to point out the jokers, the dull-heads, the ones who dared the railway crossing to relieve their boredom, and he would say that even among them, there was no such demon.

Then he felt the wind stop.

He straightened up, flicking off the torch. The sun dazzled him, swollen and red at the top of the hill. He swivelled away, saw Alfie on the dozer, laboring on another pass. But his eyes were still dazzled, because the yellow machine seemed to shimmer, ringed in a distortion of light. He turned further, gazing back down the valley to where the striker was parked next to the dam. Bella, Alfie's forty-year-old daughter, was up to her hips in brown water, placing the inlet for the pump.

"Wind's dropped!" Rory said. "Maybe we'll get a break, eh?"

Maybe I'll get home tonight, Mark thought, and see Chrissie and Jo. He smiled, picturing the two blonde heads—at three years old, Jo was the curlier and giggled more often—and his wife's relieved smile. They could all return to the residence attached to the Fairlie Public School, where half a bottle of Fairlie Grove shiraz, a big, cool bath and a big, clean bed awaited him. The passing smoke slowed and spread, as a breeze puffed gently, cooling his back even through the protective jacket.

He was facing south now. His back was towards the north. The cool became a chill.

"Rory," he said, "turn off your torch. I think the wind is *shifting.*"

Then there was a blast of heat and, he would swear, a screaming, howling sound as the northerly hit. Dust stung his face and when he looked north, in place of the trees beyond the break he saw a billow of dense, black smoke. Too close, was all he could think, that's the main fire but it's way too close! And it's coming—shit, it's coming *here*!

"Go!' Rory bellowed as a new noise, a frizzling, crackling rose. "Down to the dam!"

Mark started to run, and that was the moment old Alfie threw himself off the seat of the dozer and headed across the new-dug furrows. But his foot caught and he tripped, sprawling across the scar. Rory was several metres ahead of Mark, thanks to his greater mass: he bellowed, altering course towards Alfie. Mark hesitated just a second, then followed suit. Old he might be, but Alfie was heavy.

Then something burst on his ears and shoved him in the chest.

Mark only knew that somehow the earth was under his back and the sky above his face, but the smoke must have cleared from the sun because everything was now a brilliant and sickening yellow.

"Alf!" Rory screamed—Mark rolled and was crawling downhill, the drip torch gone from his hand, the stink of diesel penetrating his mask, the ground beneath him horribly warm. Pain accompanied the shapes forming in his field of vision. An infernal halo surrounded the dozer and, within, the blackened struts and panels all looked broken and wrong. On the ground close by, something thrashed and burned.

A hand caught his, hauled him up. "Go!"

And then Rory was hurtling straight towards the horror.

There was a hiss like an intake of breath, and smoke filled the valley like a chimney.

Mark turned and pelted in the direction of Bella and the striker. Within steps he was blind again and the smoke pierced his nostrils—his mask had come loose. Rather than stop, he held his breath as he kept stumbling down, down, and as his foot skidded and hit wet, his vision cleared: in the pocket of air above the dam surface he saw Bella in the muddy water, holding the hose aloft and training a steady, light shower on the striker.

The water embraced him. It took his weight and replaced the smoke inside his leaking mask. "Bella," he croaked, "Alfie, I saw—"

He saw.

All around him, the massive trunks of trees climbing to foliage, sinking roots into the dam and crowding every side of the valley. Giant, old growth trees, every detail of bark and leaf etched in crimson and charcoal, and all the myriad shades that fire placed between. A fretwork of saplings, underbrush, flowers and fallen logs spread in every direction.

Then in a moment they were fading, gone like forgetting. Fading to grey ash and smoke plumes. On the western hill, there was still a suggestion of trunks etched across the bare and smouldering ground, but otherwise it resembled a giant coal heap, their pathetic back-burn lost amid the universal char. The fire had passed.

The fire had passed and the striker stood, apparently unaffected, save for the black clots adhering to the damp windshield and scarlet sides. Bella was sloshing towards the bank. "Rory!" she called. Then, "Papa!"

Mark followed her, the dreadful words still hovering on his tongue, *I saw him burn.* Spot fires were eating away at the eastern hill, drifts of embers winked redly across the valley floor, but to his amazement there was still grass under the truck and around the dam. The fire front had not been broken by their efforts, but it had swerved.

It was heading *south.* It was heading towards Fairlie, where Chrissie was making sandwiches and dispensing iced water at brigade HQ, while Jo played around her feet.

"Papa!" Bella's cry rang through the mirk.

"Radio!" Rory's voice was an agonised rasp.

The air against Mark's face was still hot but his insides were stone cold as he staggered up the gluey, broken clay of the bank. As Rory staggered out of the smoke, a grisly burden over his shoulders, Mark headed for the striker, pulling off his gloves. The metal of the door handle was uncomfortably warm: he yanked the door open and hauled himself inside. Thank god, the radio unit was still showing all the right lights: he grabbed the handset and tore off his mask and goggles. "This is striker calling HQ, do you copy?"

HQ was the Fairlie community centre, where Megan Grant, the Captain's wife, would be hunched at the radio, directing operations. But the atonal crackling did not change and no voice replied. "This is striker calling HQ, the front has jumped the break."

Mark scrabbled inside his jacket for his mobile. He had speed-dialed Chris before realising he had no signal. But he *had* to reach her, had to know that she had taken Jo and evacuated (as was the plan) to Tamworth. Yes, he knew she hadn't been happy with the idea, had insisted on staying to help, but she had promised if the wind changed... would there be time? *Could* she get out? With some crazed idea of clambering on top of the vehicle (when obviously, the mobile tower had gone down and it would make no difference), he threw the door open just as Bella called for light. He hit the headlamps.

Mark had done his training, of course he had. He had seen the videos of car wrecks and looked at the pictures of burn injuries. He had read the manuals and not one of them had mentioned the smell, or the sounds Alfie was now making. His moustache was gone, along with his brows and lashes. In the filmy light his lips were one, white blister and though his pants and jacket were intact, Mark thought bad things had happened beneath them.

"Diesel vapour," husked Rory. He was covered in dirt and ash. "Tank must have been leaking. Then when the wind changed, it carried sparks."

"We've got to move," said Mark, turning back to the striker. "I'll go cross-country, I'll find help."

"We all go." Bella did not raise her head, busy with spray and gauze. "And we pack the hose away first."

***

Joining the volunteer brigade had been Chrissie's idea. Brought up outside of Bathurst, she understood these country towns and knew that, though teachers were respected, they were still outsiders. Intruders into a tightly-knit community.

"The brigade's a way of showing we're committed to living here," she had said, Jo burbling happily in her lap. "My Dad was still doing it when he was seventy-four."

Which may or may not have been the best recommendation, but Mark had grown up in the very heart of Sydney city. He was all at sea in a place where the largest business was the pub and the second the feed and hardware store, and either building was larger than the school he had signed on to run. So he followed her advice, met Captain Grant, Alfie and Bella, Rory and all the others. Rory had a daughter in year seven and a two-year-old son, and his wife and Chrissie became fast friends. And he came to enjoy the meetings in the little plaster hall, with its flaking, white walls and clustering pepper trees. On weekends, they would do training exercises in the car park.

Now he was driving the striker as fast as he dared along the fire trail that looped around the eastern hill, retracing their steps of an hour? Two hours previous? In smoke like strands of solid night, weaving through the blackened stands of eucalypts. The leaves hadn't burned. The fire had sucked the oil out of them and leapt right on. The ice in his gut was still demanding he floor it, but both Rory and Bella insisted upon caution. "Even on the trail there'll be embers," she said, "Go over a burn, we'll lose the tyres and that will be that, and a prayer."

Alfie lay across the back seat, wrapped in a thermal blanket with his head in Bella's lap. How was she doing it? Mark gripped the wheel. Why wasn't she screaming?

There on the left, he saw live fire; orange-red blossoms hanging from trees in the premature darkness. Alongside the track lay nests of red coals, the collapsed remains of ferns or brush. The smoke was getting thicker, caught in the striker's headlamps. In the light from the dash, steam rose from his damp clothes.

"We better stop," said Rory, but Mark wasn't listening.

Mark *saw* the girl.

At first, it looked like part of the trail, a patch of paler earth. Then earth resolved into a girl with hair like flame, running through the scorched night. For a long moment he watched her, understanding nothing, then realised that the trees were back, the centuries-old giants with their shaggy bark and buttress roots, limned in orange and grey.

As the striker rolled forward, she came into focus. Her hair wasn't red, it was a rich black-brown with gold strands, but somehow, it glowed. Her skin was brown and held that same luminous quality. She was wearing a short dress of nondescript colour and shape, and her legs were bare. Her only protection was a pair of flat shoes, pressing into the ashes.

Then suddenly, a massive shoulder pushed past him and the tyres spun against sand, as Rory jammed on the brake. The striker coasted to a stop just short of the blackened remains of a fallen tree.

Mark could still see the girl, her dress fluttering where any cloth would burst into flames, stepping on charcoal as hot as a stove. The strands of her hair not kindling as she ran straight into the ancient forest. But then, none of those trees were burned at all.

"For eff's sake, man!" Rory extricated himself.

Mark's voice wavered. "Did you see her? Did you?"

"It's nothing." Bella's voice was flat. "A phantom."

"A phantom?"

"Like those you see on the side of the road, when you drive at night for too long."

"Oh, a mirage," said Mark. The distinction between the words suddenly seemed very important: he could imagine himself describing it to a class. *A mirage is an optical illusion formed when rising heat causes an atmospheric refraction, whereas to call something a phantom or spectre implies belief in a supernatural origin...*

Rory pulled his mask up. "I'll go out and clear it."

Chrissie and Jo. "No, no need for that. We can take the truck round to the right: look, it's quite flat—"

"No," said Bella. In her lap, Alfie made an odd, mewling sound.

No one suggested Mark get out and help, so he didn't, remained there with his hands glued to the wheel. That they were just sitting here, in the midst of all this, was impossible: how fast had the fire been going, to jump them like that? And why the hell hadn't the main crew radioed them to update the fire's position, or responded when he called?

Because they couldn't. Which was a ridiculous thought, but that didn't stop terror closing his parched throat.

Alfie mewled again.

"Shush Papa," Bella murmured, "I'm here."

At last, Rory clambered back inside, bringing a fresh wave of smoke. Mark focused on the trail through the soot-scabbed windscreen and nursed the striker on.

"We don't have any native people in Fairlie," said Rory, apparently by way of conversation. "Used to be a what? A reservation? That became the reserve. But they were all gone by then."

Mark found himself latching onto the distraction. He *had* heard about the reservation and how the First Australians living there had worked on the cattle stations, until such time as they didn't. In the function rooms of Fairlie Glen Estate, sepia photos included contingents of dark-skinned men and women that never made the transition to greyscale; replaced, when the vines arrived, by Alfie's kin. He wondered what had actually happened to them. Wondered if Chrissie had remembered to collect the lockbox with their passports and Jo's birth certificate.

And then the darkness peeled away and through the windscreen, he saw the flat expanse of the paddocks surrounding Fairlie—desolate in the rufous light—and four blessed lanes of blacktop.

But then Rory placed one meaty hand on his arm and he was forced to halt again, just short of the sign announcing "HISTORIC FAIRLIE GLEN ESTATE 40K". They would not let him budge until he tried the radio again.

"Striker to HQ... Regional, *anybody*?"

Then he swivelled around to face Bella. "They'll all be at Fairlie," he said. "Ambulances too."

After a long moment, Bella nodded.

Mark hit the accelerator. The wheels screamed as he swerved onto the road, then he gunned it as hard as he could.

Out the driver's window, he saw hills burning under a blood red sky. Great, black fingers groped over the ridge, down gully and fence line, offspring of the spot fires they hadn't stayed to put out (and not even Bella had suggested that.) To the east, the paddocks whipped by. The grass and fringing poplars were thick with ash: it was almost like snow. It was hard to imagine anything had ever lived here. Telegraph poles looped monotonously: if those creeping, licking fingers reached them, there would simply be more ash. Bursts of the stuff crossed the road in front of him: how many times had he driven this stretch in his own vehicle with Chrissie beside him and Jo strapped into her car seat in the back?

In the back seat, Bella's voice had the cadence of prayer.

Then up ahead (still distant, but closing by the second), Mark saw a bright light. Within heartbeats, it resolved into the same sulphurous glow as had enveloped the dozer. An accident, someone in this sifting smoke had come off the road. Fuck, would he have to stop *again*?

Now there was the shape of a cabin and long, cylindrical body, and what he had not realised (putting everything down to their own speed), was that the flaming truck was speeding towards them, shedding that terrible light.

"Jesus!" Bella yelped. "Get off the road!"

Mark swerved. Bella gasped. He felt the striker shudder and swing over the gravel verge, as the roar of the oncoming tanker (a *fuel* tanker, dear god!) swallowed all sound, like the bushfire as it swept through the valley, glowing like the dozer had glowed but to Mark's eye, cabin and tank were intact right down to the tyres, down to the side mirror and scrolling crimson and yellow logo.

Then it was past them and the complaint of their tyres on the verge crackled in his ears and he slowed.

"Rory?" Bella quavered.

"Yeah," husked Rory. "Yeah, it was."

"Were you expecting a delivery?" asked Mark. His arms were shaking, as he steered them back onto the road.

In the rear vision mirror, Bella shook her head. "Back in the nineties, when we were kids, both our Dads were in the fire service."

"Yeah." Though Rory was covered in soot and smut, he sounded pale. "This one time, they got called out to where a tanker had rolled on the highway. We came out too, to see. By the time we got there, it had caught fire." Mark didn't take his eyes off the road; he was counting now, the little landmarks, the sign posts and letter boxes closing in on the turn off.

"We all saw the dozer go up," he said. "Then we saw this stupid trucker go by, in this shitty light—" With a logo, he realised, he hadn't seen since the nineties, but that couldn't be right. "It's just another mirage."

"It's nothing," Bella said, "But it may mean something."

FAIRLIE 20K

***

And of course, they'd all been worried about nothing.

As they crossed the railway line, it looked bad, but that was mostly smoke and ash. A few of the outlying buildings had caught: the odd, old cottage and farm shed that no one could be bothered to save. They were smouldering still and, in the Grant's orchard, each tree bore a heavy crop of flame.

But the further they got into town, the more obvious it was to Mark that he'd been right. Whether by the main brigade with the tanker or through the efforts of the residents, wielding sack and garden hose, the fire had been repelled. Of course it had! Towns didn't *burn*. Even towns like this.

As they rolled down the main street past the shuttered shops, the silence was certainly eerie and the sky above them opened and closed like a volcanic rift. Black ash drifted down the pavement, wound through the wrought iron pillars supporting the pub's balcony, and anyone without a mask would obviously be inside.

"This isn't right," said Bella, "Doesn't feel right."

"They're all at the community centre," said Mark. Did it really take an outsider to tell these people what was what? He kept on coasting down the road, alert for trucks and ambulances, or people flagging him down. Here and there, in the corner of his eye, he caught feral glints in gutters or drifting down side streets, but knew these had to be reflections, the blood red light bouncing back from car mirrors or windows. The windows of the school. As he approached the corner of Bell Street, he gave a kind of chuckle. There was enough smoke up there that something must have caught: now Rory would definitely blame the kids. But the fact was, he didn't care: the residence had never been his home and the school itself barely more than a workplace.

A career move, to come here, even if his wife believed it a fit place to raise their child.

"Ave Maria," Bella prayed, "Gratia plena." Alfie hadn't made a sound now, in several minutes.

Suddenly, there was a popping and a thump he felt through floor and door; the striker dropped a full inch and shuddered. They did not stop but their progress slowed to a chunk-a-chunk crawl.

"That was the tyres," said Rory.

What did he want Mark to do? Stop and change them? The noise and heavy steering were annoying, and the cabin seemed to be heating up, but they were so close to where Alfie could be handed over to the proper authorities and there'd be tears but cheers as well, for after all the entire striker unit could have died spritzing water down the fire's throat.

Once again, steam rose from his clothes.

Would Chrissie be there, or had she gone? It didn't matter, not truly: his need to see her was an ache in his chest, but it would be satisfying too, had she gone. Because he was a teacher and she was a teacher, and for all their talk, they were never seriously going to stay.

A pall of smoke blocked him like some final test and Rory kept his damn hands to himself. He pushed the striker into it, through it, and suddenly, there it was.

He saw.

The community centre stood amid the pepper trees, with not a single char on its white surface. The curling, ferny leaves were green. And there in the car park were the people and at their centre, Chrissie stood with Jo in her arms, her face fairly glowing with joy, all of them radiant. Megan, Rory's wife, a group of boys from his class: all the people who'd stayed to man the radio and make sure that whenever the firies returned, there'd be water and sandwiches, and a warm embrace.

What he couldn't see was any trace of the tanker crew. No helmets or jackets: no, wait, there was the uncanny shimmer of reflective tape. A man stood at the front of the crowd, gloved and helmeted, frowning and pointing towards the striker as if to say, what the hell are you doing?

Alfie. That man was Alfie.

Mark jammed on the brakes.

And then, as the fire raged on south and the heat loosed its grip on the remains of Fairlie, the mirage faded. As the ancient trees had faded, along with the truck and the fleeing girl. The glow went first, beloved faces fading to ash, then the outlines of flesh and hair dissolving, revealing what truly lay beyond. The devastation of brickwork and timber, smoking trees, the burning cars with bodies inside, caught as they tried to flee.

As Rory dragged his mask up over his face and Bella gently set her father down, Mark screamed and screamed.

Welcoming the End

Aura Redwood

Adversity brings out the best in people. It can also bring out the weird, the absurd, and the just plain crazy. I bought this story because not everyone reacts to natural disasters the same way.

Phyllis Irene Radford

Welcoming the End
by
Aura Redwood

"You all know why you are here today," a man dressed in fine black linen announced loudly to the ever-eager crowd. The gathering looked up to him as he stood on what had once been an awe-inspiring altar. The dilapidated chapel that they stood in, no longer had any of its former glory. The destruction and dirt created by any person who had freely wandered in made it seem less like a house of God and more a tetanus hazard.

This had not stopped the small crowd of two dozen people who had congregated. They stared, with the same reverence that was once given to a priest, at this clean-shaven man. Everyone in the area knew him only as Edward the Begetter.

"We have waited and waited as we saw the world around us decay and destroy itself. We watched what was supposed to be a blessing, be destroyed right in front of our eyes. This world is no longer the garden we were promised," Spittle flew from Edward's mouth as he started to truly get into the rhythm of his belief, "Each new day passes by and the cries for help are not heard. Each new night you watch the news and you hear about the blasphemies that man has enacted on each other. This place is no longer a home for good men. This place is no longer what we could consider our home, it truly is now finally time for Eschatos."

A sparse cheer accompanied the few hands that applauded in agreement.

"No more watching and waiting. It is now time for us to accept the glory that is Eschatos. It is time for us to leave this world behind and to be welcomed by his open arms."

A resounding cheer emitted from the crowd and filled the chapel as the raucous energy of the small flock started to rise. A light started to shine behind the sunken eyes of those that stared up at the preaching man.

"We are no longer going to live in despair and fear. We are now going to take our destiny in our own hands and bring our world into a brighter future. Eschatos will cleanse this earth and accept each and every one of us as his own children."

Eyes followed each word spoken as if it was the gospel truth and before long cheers were thundering from the small wooden chapel.

"You know what needs to be done. You know what you have to do. So now with the truth that is Eschatos, go out in the world this night and bring his light to all those who are suffering and those who know no better. Be his messenger and set this world alight."

With those final words, Edward the Begetter got off from his rotten podium and started to stride down the aisle, towards the night that had started to set upon the rural town. A bright smile upon his face, he led the women and men behind him away from the sanctuary and into the reality of his creating.

***

With a sloshing sound, the indiscriminate brown bottle reached his parched lips. He guzzled greedily on the teat that had been his reprise from a much too young age. Dirty liquor dribbled down his chin until it reached its brother stains on his shirt. Wobbling uncertainty, Jonathon got up from his chair on the old wooden deck of the old shit house he called his home.

His unsteady march down the steps left him blearily looking at the sad sight that had become his life. Brown hard dirt as far as the eye could see, everything around him but the overtaking wild bush was dead. What had once been a flourishing farm under the hands of his father and his father's father, was now a dried up and lifeless scene. He wasn't going to lie and say he was brought up in luxury, but they had done well. Well enough to be able to hire other men from the town to help them harvest the wheat and barley fields. Now though, he was all alone. All alone in the shit hole of his own making.

Throwing the bottle harshly to the hard dirt, the glass shattered into filthy speckles that landed as small mines around his feet. Jon paid no attention to the glass shards. He once again, with new vigour, trudged along. He continued his march towards the bone dry bush that enclosed his house with the large canister in his left hand. His boots kicked up dry red dirt and the cicadas sang loudly, filling his swimming head with a loud buzz. Wobbling, he stopped at the edge of the bush and his eyes blinked blankly as he looked down at the red canister.

His right hand started to unscrew the cap of the petrol canister. Reaching as high as his tired arms would let him, he let the gasoline pour down his head and slosh down soaking his clothes and boots. The cold liquid hitting his skin, made his eyes widen slightly as the smell reached his nose. Turning his head to see the fields, he then looked back at the woodlands. Where there had once been the song of the bush, there was now a thick silence as the forest looked back at him and waited in apprehension for what he was about to do.

"There is nothing left for me here"

With a sharp sound, John held a lit lighter in his hands. Before he could even have a second thought, the fire travelled up his arm and to his drenched clothes. His eyes widened but no scream escaped his mouth as his body became a large ball of flames. His shocked scream became a hardened grimace on his face and with steel cold determination he continued his march towards the parched scrub.

Within seconds, Jonathon had disappeared into the thickness of the bush leaving only the bright licking flames that jumped from his body to the vegetation like a starving dog. An agonizing scream escaped the flames, and then all that was left was the raging fire.

***

Only a little while away, Mary had left her quiet house filled with smiling faces that permanently grinned at the photographer behind the camera. Walking out into the warm evening air only dressed in a light white nightgown that clung damply to her body, she ambled towards the thicket, showing a sight that her grandchildren would turn away from with embarrassed giggles. Her bare feet padded across the barren dirt towards the line of the inviting trees as the sun started to set somewhere on the far horizon.

Her fingers unconsciously turned the golden band around her finger until she was in the middle of the bush. Dried out leaves crunched under her feet as she carefully stepped towards a clearing that sang its familiar and welcoming ballad to her tired ears. Her hands patted to her side and there she once again located the tarnished lighter that was engraved with three blackening letters TJM.

Caressing the letters lovingly, she took in a deep breath before flicking open the lighter. The old ignitor opened with a creak, showing nothing but the brass cap.

"Oh of course," She mumbled to herself, "Nothing was ever that easy was it, Tim?"

Her arthritic thumb struck the spark wheel down a few times and then a little flame lit up the area in the darkening sky. The flame did not wait for her to realise that she had been successful, instead, it rushed towards the gasoline that covered her from head to toe. The fire roared as it reached her soaked nightgown.

She looked up at the sky, a small smile growing on her face as she watched the stars coming out to greet the night.

"Finally"

Her body collapsed to the ground, her eyes closing as she accepted her final moment with only a light whimper. The leaves below helped her continue her mission and it was only a few moments until the bushes around her lit the scenery with a ferocious light.

***

Back once again, Edward stood outside the old decrepit chapel. His eyes shone as he stared at the view around him, his smile widening to the point where his lips could truly not stretch anymore. Now that the darkness of the thick smoke had started to settle upon the small town and blocked out any light of the moon and stars, the fire lit up the scenery around him as brilliantly as a thousand fireworks.

Striding towards the burning heat, he stopped in the middle of the flame-licked clearing. His arms out wide he spun around like a showman in his prime, to announce loudly to any being that could hear him.

"Eschatos, this is your time! This, this is all for you," His arms gestured wildly out to the roaring wall of flames that surrounded him from all sides. The embers of the fire jumped from shrub to grass, edging its way ever closer to him.

"Take our humble offering, all-mighty Eschatos and welcome us with open arms to your new world," Edward yelled out loudly to be heard over the breaking of trees and the rush of fire. In the background somewhere there were sirens and shouts far in the distance. He paid no heed though and welcomed the fire as it reached him, a tidal wave of flame pushed through him and swallowed his withering and shrivelling body whole.

The lands were now ablaze with fire too bright to look at. The disciples themselves consumed by that which they worshipped, leaving only the fiery death that longed to reach all edges of the land. Scrambling bodies of both humans and animals tried their best to escape the flames. If one had stayed still and silent though, maybe just maybe if they were truly listening to the world around them, they would have heard the low rumble of a chuckle as the fire started to take hold.

OZ is Burning

Beef

Zena Shapter

This story was inspired by my deep appreciation of and respect for nature, as well as an acknowledgement of the fragility of our modern lives–at any moment, everything familiar to us could be gone.

Zena Shapter

Beef
by
Zena Shapter

The plants grew so fast they ripped through roads as we drove across them, pulsing beneath concrete like veins under thin skin. Parks and reserves furred over cities and towns, suffocating supplies and communications, then feasted at their leisure. Burning them would have burnt us all. We had no choice but to ignore the screams and try up the coast.

A retirement village had two outdoor pools covered in leaf litter. They stank of damp dirt and rotting mango flesh, but seemed quiet enough. Aunty Jean, our best gardener, suggested chlorine as the reason. Other survivors joined us. But one night snappy lean palms bent into bedrooms while we slept. Algae blooms slurped up sea life. Spores smothered the unmasked. We left everything and sprinted for our utes.

Those who survived fled for the outback. Aunty Jean was certain this time – the lack of water would act as a barrier for anything cellulose, keep us safe.

She was right. Ghost gums and mulga reached for us so slowly we could easily dodge and cut them back. Woody shrubs spiked through the cracked earth, then wilted under the heat. Lethargic jabs of their twiggy stems did little more than scratch when we chopped them down for burning at night. Dared we dream the desert our sanctuary?

Outcrops of exposed bedrock were best for sleeping; roots couldn't sneak under soil and surprise us. We salvaged what we could, made shelters from rocks, old cars, torn cloth. We hunted other animals seeking refuge under the suffocating sun, the dusty dry air slowing them too.

We missed vegetables of course, fruit. Farms and stations dotted across the flat land tempted us with their billowing green canopies of produce, thriving thanks to deep-dug wells no human could ever use again. Jean said it wasn't worth the risk. She was cultivating a small garden of basil and lettuce, hoping to control it soon enough, though struggled with the correct balance of sand, soil and clay, or something like that. I never was much good at horticulture.

Your father and I were doing okay anyway, roasting birds, bats, snakes and goannas... until you came along.

It was my fault, I suppose, because it was my milk that dried up. I should have asked for extra water rations. But we didn't know better – you were our first and no one else had children. Even myall trees grew faster than most of the families who'd tried to flee.

You became so thirsty, undernourished. Still the milk wouldn't come. We tried stewing bilby chunks and flaky strings of lizard flesh. You had no teeth to chew.

Rumours whispered of a settlement across the ridge with solar power and a blender, but you wouldn't have made the journey. You were getting so weak, your limbs bony, your chest barely rising as you inhaled trembling gasps of hot breath. Sweat glistened on your tiny forehead.

The Durham's old station was so close we could see it – a vibrant smudge of colour that licked the horizon like dog spew. Your father reckoned he was fast enough on his feet to try it. He had long legs. All we needed was a potato to mash up, a banana or pumpkin – something, anything moist and nutritious that you could digest.

I walked him most of the way. The station's scraggly canopy of desert oaks thickened. Its dense understorey of wattle hid weatherboard buildings. Pale pointy grasses stood to attention, guarding the perimeter. A breeze carried scents of watermelon and tomatoes.

"She'll never know bread," he said as we walked around it, searching for a way inside. Every day he'd think of a different food to miss. "Or steak."

"Grains need fields," was all I could think to say. "Cows need grass."

"I know."

The creaking of bark made us both freeze. "Is it a Gripper or Carnie?" By then we knew the two species worked together.

"Shh!" he hissed, though plants don't have ears.

Still, we said goodbye in whispers, just in case. It must've been our instincts warning us, some subconscious acknowledgement of a truth we weren't ready to face.

Leaves had always rustled.

Branches had always clicked.

Of course plants knew how to talk.

Now they had learnt our language, they'd figured out how we thrived, and wanted the same for themselves.

Your father did what he could – crept quietly through the scrub, low to the ground like it would keep him out of sight. A dirt track led into the property, wide enough for five people, and at its end among the foliage an aluminium roof glinted, as did the unsmashed glass of windows underneath. He took his time, watching for movement.

Not even a leaf fluttered.

It wasn't until he was a hundred or so metres down the track that a stretching sound groaned across the groundcover, like taut plastic wrap. He turned to run back but grasses grew like a flash-floor across the dirt, barricading him.

He ran across it anyway, his sprint becoming a wade as stems bound his shins and wouldn't let go.

"Stay back!" he yelled at me. He must have seen the Gripper vines twisting towards him. "Don't look!"

I couldn't turn away. Tears still wet my face when I think of him. He loved you so much. But we didn't know back then. There was a reason we'd called theirs a kingdom, equal to ours. We shouldn't have fed them so much blood and bone.

If only Jean had realised sooner that we could harvest and mush the flesh of prickly pears as baby food. If only someone had realised what plants wanted, before that day.

But we didn't.

We know now, thanks to your father – as the vines carried him struggling into the station, branches parted to reveal a sandy clearing of people, old and young, all naked, standing huddled and whimpering. They saw me but didn't move or try to escape. Then the bushes closed together once more, blocking them from view, fencing them in like a herd.

Like a herd.

The grasses retreated, leaving the dirt track wide open once more, tempting, luring, trapping. Because that's what they do now, and will always do, little one, that's why I'm writing this all down – so you'll always remember: the plants wanted control and now they have it.

We are the cows now.

The Last Wish

Lauren E. Mitchell

Wishing in fiction tends to lead to that 'ha ha, sucked in' moment where the protagonist miswords something by the tiniest bit and the wish-granter gleefully twists it to harm them. I wanted to write a story where the outcome was exactly what the protagonist wanted and that ha-ha moment got turned back on the wish-granter.

Lauren E. Mitchell

The Last Wish
by
Lauren E. Mitchell

The woman cracked open her soft drink can and raised it to her mouth. Instead of the anticipated sweetness and caffeine, she found herself coughing as a gaseous cloud rebounded off her tongue to hover midair a metre away. The cloud reshaped itself from an undefined blob into a humanoid shape, wearing curly-toed slippers, a turban, and flowing robes.

'Surprise,' said the genie.

'Last week the vending machine stole my money. This week I get a can of djinn and no tonic.' The woman paused and looked levelly at the genie. 'I don't suppose there's any chance you'd just go away?'

'If you wish.'

'I very specifically do not.' The woman was sitting in the garden where she often ate her lunch. Around it rose tall buildings, their glass windows reflecting the grey smoke haze above back and forth. The grass was short. Some of it was so short it was just dirt. In the dirt were rocks and cigarette butts and an empty chip packet. The garden abutted St. Francis' Church, but not even the sparrows looked enthused about it.

'You know the drill, I see,' said the genie, poking at the dirt with one slippered toe and grimacing.

'Aladdin was one of the first movies I saw at the cinema. I sat in the third row from the front. My neck hurt from craning back by the end.' The woman shook her soft drink can hopefully, but it didn't even remotely slosh. 'Why this?' She shook it again at the genie. 'What happened to the lamp?'

'These days the only people who look at old brass lamps are antiques dealers. Do you know the sorts of things they wish for? I got tired of dust and sand and bringing back the Great Library of Alexandria only for someone else to wish it away again.'

'It seems counterintuitive to have one wish eradicate the wishes of others.'

'I don't make the rules,' said the genie. 'I just follow them. What one master wishes, the next master might find utterly antithetical to their way of life.'

'I can't say I ever heard about the return of the Great Library on the news.'

'That's the thing about modern society. It's so fast-paced. Three wishes and I'm recycled for the next person without so much time as a hashtag to start trending.'

'That's just what we live with in a capitalist society.' The woman finally gave up on the can and unwrapped her sandwich instead, pausing to lift the top slice of bread to check for other supernatural manifestations before taking a bite. 'I'm surprised you don't at least get a few tweets though.'

'Who says I don't? It just goes away again when the next wish resets the world. Do you know how many times the world's ended just in the last year?'

'Let me guess. People fixing climate change, famine, unequal distribution of wealth...' The genie nodded along with the woman's words. 'World peace.'

At that last, a look of hunger came over the genie's face, and the woman hid her smile behind her sandwich.

'It's such a pretty dream. So many people have it. Would you like to try? You can always undo it again with your second wish.' The genie's eyes glittered with avarice.

The woman inclined her head slightly, checked the time on her phone, and said, 'Why not? I still have fifteen minutes' lunch break left. I wish for world peace.'

The constant sound of traffic on Lonsdale Street stopped. The voices of worshippers entering and exiting St. Francis' Church stopped. The voice of the Big Issue vendor on the corner was cut off mid-spruik.

And the genie was outright laughing now. 'You humans are all alike. You all fall for that one. Boy, you should see your—' The genie stopped, because the woman didn't look shocked or distraught or any of the expected reactions.

Instead, the woman merely said, 'You got tired of being crammed into lamps and curled into rings. You got tired of being reduced to words on a page. You got tired of being perceived differently by different cultures.' The woman met the genie's eyes. '2400 BCE, wasn't it, when they started talking about you in Arabia? Forgive me if I don't know exactly when every other culture decided to borrow you, although I know Disney's version dates to 1992 CE.'

'All those thousands of years.'

'Good, evil, trickster spirit, strict logician, rules lawyer.' The woman finished her sandwich and rolled the cling-wrap into a ball, tucking it into her pocket. 'Thousands of years, hundreds of perceptions, once being voiced by Robin Williams...'

'That part wasn't so bad,' the genie conceded.

'It must get confusing, being so many things to so many different people.'

'You have no idea.'

'No,' the woman said. 'I don't. Because I have only ever been one thing to everyone. All I have ever been to all of humankind is their mother.' She stood up, stretched, and stepped on the soft drink can, flattening it.

'You—'

The woman bent and picked up the crushed can. 'I have tried for so long not to choose between my children, whether they were humans or dinosaurs or amoebae.' She looked around again at Melbourne's cityscape, towering into the dismal smoke-hazed sky, dug deep into the ground, spread out over the earth. 'But these children have done so much damage with their toys, even the ones with which they meant no harm.'

'You—'

'Thank you,' said the woman. 'I appreciate you offering me the chance for my peace.'

She left the garden with the gate standing open; there were no people now to further fill it with rubbish, and there might be wildlife that would appreciate the thin grass, the meagre flowers, and the struggling, defiant trees.

Writing on the Wall

Gillian Polack

I was stuck at home in one room dreaming of an outside world, the air purifier working overtime. That was my bushfire summer. Like our COVID year, but with smoke and less space. It came to me that this experience was perfect for a story that told a bit more about what happened behind the scenes in my novel, *The Year of the Fruit Cake.* You don't have to read one to understand the other. Some of the mysteries of each, however, are less mysterious when you read both. How mysterious do you want your universe, that is the question.

Gillian Polack

Writing on the Wall
by
Gillian Polack

This is not the way the world was supposed to end. I'm in a house surrounded by dark. A small house. A safe house. For now.

I've written so many stories about the end of the world. I've mocked TS Eliot ending the world with a whimper. Last time I tried to leave by the front door, I ducked back inside far too quickly, whimpering. I will not mock TS Eliot again.

I have written about the Terminator and apocalypses where Schwarzenegger comes to save us. There is no us. There is only me. Arnie will not come.

I need to stop dwelling on the possible and stop dreaming of my little stories. They brought me a tiny bit of glory in the day, but I honestly didn't know Armageddon. I enjoyed imagining an end of the world, but I didn't believe it was possible.

I was stupid. We were all stupid. In denial. I made jokes about that, too. "Like Pharaoh," I said, "In denial."

The reality is everyday and ordinary and numb and slow and safe and... it's the end of everything. The worst part of it is that I'm powerless. My stories can't save me.

I just caught myself yawning. This isn't the story I want to tell now. The end of everything is boring. This story is particularly dull. The thing is, this story is true.

***

I was talking to a group of writing friends before everything went dark. We'd been told that we should write about past and present in equal measure. The instructions were waiting for us when we came to this 'retreat'. One of the writers said she'd write about her childhood.

"Nice idea," said my ex, who most unfortunately had also got a place for this so-special creative group. "I can write about my birth. Squalling as I was ripped from the womb. It probably hurt a hell of a lot more than now, but I was alive and had so many things ahead. That's the kind of story I should write now," he said.

I played quiet. My mind was arguing with all of them, but I didn't say a thing. I had white masks in my bag. Two of them. Class P2. We all had at least one mask in our bag. That was why we were meeting before we settled into our fortnight of funded literature. The news had told us about the shadow over the world and we thought it was something to do with bushfires so we had all prepared. We read out arrival instructions and discussed them and the masks and the shadow. Then the shadow went away and we decided to stay together for dinner. The only masks we needed were the ones we put on to write about characters experiencing the end of the world. Our first-person-pretend masks.

This is like *On the Beach*. Quiet preparations for the end of the world, then knowing it will never come, then it comes even more quietly than our preparations.

Quietude comes quietly. The darkness will hover over capital cities. City by city. We didn't know this when we sat together, that first afternoon.

I went to my small writerly room after our chat and I thought, "This room needs books." That was the first thing I wrote in this journal.

I woke up at home. I must've gone home after the meeting, because I woke up there. I did. I'm not sure I'm at home now. All my books are here, at least, but the darkness has been outside for five days and five nights. My computer measures the time for me. It tells me I have been here for five days and five nights. And yet that eternal blackness lifted before I went home. I came indoors by moonlight and woke up to... no outside, only inside.

Does it sound as if I'm making things up? I wish I were. Does it sound as if I'm confused and even tangled? I most certainly am. My mind is out of joint.

The lights came back on but outside remained dark and, ever since then, I've sounded very certain and know that my certainty is fake. I tell myself I'm dreaming, and that gets me through. I tell myself that I watch too many horror movies, but I don't watch horror movies at all.

I hate the dark. I hate it so very much.

I've been on the computer a lot. My computer contained some new files and I was stupid and explored them. If they had contained a virus I would have been stuffed.

In a way, they did contain a virus and I was very stuffed. The files were maps showing me what the dark was doing to Earth. I was fascinated by the movement of the dark. I took all the files and gifs and everything else and I married them together and discovered the pattern of apocalypse. Darkness ate cities then regions then whole countries and finally the whole globe would be dark. The files were in English and they contained timelines. We have twenty years left.

I can't access social media at all, but for three days I could email some of my friends. Not all my friends. Just the group that was supposed to be on a retreat with me. They had experienced what I'd experienced and that made me feel normal. Maybe only normal within certain values, but normal. We'd all woken up at home and then realised it wasn't home at all.

The others didn't bother with the maps of Earth. Not their thing. We may all be writers, but we all write differently and enjoy wildly disparate inspiration. That's what my ex said, when I tried to explain the importance of those maps and that data to him and the rest of our little group.

We reminded each other of the time and told each other to eat or to go to sleep. When we muddled back online together, we developed theory after theory for what had happened. Not what would happen. Just the past. We decided that we were all at home (maybe), but none of us remember having returned there. My ex complained that he couldn't go outside to get his lawnmower back from a neighbour. Mowing the lawn was not on anyone else's mind.

The darkness outside poisons all our thoughts. Even those of my ex, who decided that weedkiller would do for his lawn and went to his garage if he had any. He didn't. He didn't have to go outside to reach the garage. He didn't try for his shed. He didn't say this, but that would've taken him outside. Into the dark.

Eventually we admitted to each other that we were being managed by someone or something. The maps and the diagrams and the reports had been given to us by those who reach through the darkness.

I might be imagining that end. I imagine so many things now that all I have is my three-bedroom house without a backyard or a front yard or a view. I've tried imagining this situation as an intelligent cloud that envelopes us and keeps us separate and brings us towards the end, step by step, but it's hard to animate darkness. Maybe it's where aliens who live in burrows like wombats and who think the dark was a natural and good thing. Those were my idea. All the others suggested that we live in a horror story. That there will be an end and that each step will be worse than the step before. I don't watch horror films and I'm not a horror writer. Unlike my ex who is all kinds of things. He didn't understand the dark, though. He ought to have, but he didn't.

Anyhow, the moment we realised that we were a group and that strange things were happening, my last communication outside my home was cut off. I had my books and my computer, but no people. I was alone in the world.

I was bored. I am still bored. But two days ago, when I was not quite as bored as I am now, I made plans. I wanted to reach out through my machine and let every human being know what their stories held. I wanted to, and maybe I could and yet I didn't tell them. I couldn't tell them. I looked at the maps and data that showed the advent of encompassing dark and I realised that I could parse it. The world was going to be destroyed in twenty years, by whoever was controlling our small writerly lives. Whoever? Whatever? I didn't know.

I know which cities will be eaten by darkness first and which will be the last cities alive. I even know the name of the last suburb within the last city. It terrifies me. It makes me so scared to know the path the darkness will take as it eats our world.

I am in Melbourne. It doesn't feel like Melbourne anymore because I'm confined to my smaller-than-average home. *On the Beach* is my everyday except that it isn't as pleasant as Nevil Shute said. It is also a lot duller than he said.

There are no poison pills to hasten an ending. I have knives in my kitchen, but I don't want them. I wouldn't want the poison, either. I want the companionable death Shute told us about. I want to walk on the beach one last time, with friends or with a lover or with a child running and screaming as if tomorrow were real. I want the community Shute promised us.

I want someone to save me. If I can't have a sweet companionable ending, I want someone to save me. I don't mind if there are challenges after the saving. I would welcome being thrust into space and the wonder and the danger and the unknown future, just as long as there was a future.

Or I want to walk into the good night, at the time of my choice. I want this night to be a good night. I look out the window and I see the black cloud swirling and know that this night is pure evil.

I tried walking into it. The darkness swirls and sings and reminds me of what happens. It's taking us one by one because it relishes us. It sings each of us to sleep, as if we were being brought into a joyous fold. Except we know that's not what's happening.

Let me put it all together the way I parsed those maps. To do this, I have to go back to the dinner, then to go back further still. I have to find out where it started for us.

The dinner wasn't random, nor were the gas masks.

We thought it was a trick.

The advertisement said that it was a plan to get writers to be more creative. It was funded, and I thought I could write a few stories under direction. I applied for a retreat. I won the whole shebang, everything was covered, so I agreed to come and write what the organisers suggested we write. I travelled here by bus and train and tram from the other end of Melbourne.

We brought what we thought we needed. The gas masks were because this place is near the bush and there is fire. They were something we needed, even if we didn't know that. That sounded fair to me.

In the bus on the way, I looked out the window. The whole world looked soft. The sunlight looked as if it was late in the day when it was morning, and the hills were wreathed in the most delicate grey mist. Except that the mist was smoke, and not that safe to breathe. One writer came and promptly left again. He couldn't handle the smoke.

That was the beginning. Now, what has changed since then?

Two days ago, I found I had twelve masks. Why? What would we need more masks for?

What we thought of at once was that it was to help with this summer and these fires... it felt as if the world were ending.

I had dinner with my fellow creatives and we ate much pasta and drank much red wine and sang raucously and celebrated who we were and what we would do and talked about ourselves as if ourselves were the whole universe. We separated and slept, and I woke up in the middle of the night and opened my front door and the world was not there.

I'm repeating myself. I haven't found any solutions. It's easier to parse maps than to parse experiences.

I'm still bored, aren't I? I'm going to bed. I can write more tomorrow. Tomorrow and tomorrow and tomorrow. I hope I dream tonight. I don't need more boredom.

***

It's tomorrow and things have changed.

We have been saved. I think.

I woke up to a message on this machine and an instruction to keep writing this journal. Someone likes this journal. The bit about the journal was in a footnote. The rest of the message was to all of us, except for the missing writer. I know it was all of us and not a single person beyond, for the message included each and every name, lovingly.

We were told what we had been saved for. Part of it was described to us as lovingly as our names had been listed.

These people say, "You may consider us as aliens."

They are very polite, but they frighten me. They believe in a sweet death for the species they exterminate. That was the darkness I saw creeping over Earth. Their plans for its future.

They chose us to chronicle events and to tell stories about the people they are killing. Humans. They will restore our access to the web so that we can watch Earth die.

Australia was their favourite continent because it most matched the needs of their species, so we were the people saved. They were sorry we had so few genders, another afternote said, and had no idea how to experience life as it should be experienced. Sorry. For genders. Not for killing our entire race.

Extermination the civilised way. We leave last, when our stories are finished, I assume. That's not what they said, though. They said that we remain and tell our stories. Except that I opened that door and was tempted to walk into that good night and I discovered that the night was not good. Is not good. It has eaten the air around my studio and the ground beneath it and I nearly died. Three days later I nearly died because I have been alone for too long eating food from tins. Now I'm chronicling with a vengeance and it is all too present and I want to see the sky and breathe and know that I'm merely nightmared.

I have miscounted the days, haven't I? I've read back, and none of my counting adds up.

I have a television as well as a computer. A cupboard full of food. Three tin openers. A refrigerator full of bottles of water. And air. So much air. It comes from nowhere, this air.

The garbage is emptied, and the fridge and cupboard restocked every fourth night, while I'm asleep. The plumbing behaves exactly as it should.

When I try staying awake to see where it all comes from, I fail, miserably. A drugged mist creeps under the door and it makes me sleep. The first time I saw it, I watched it come and tried to escape it by clambering onto the top of the big wardrobe. My giant nineteenth century atrocity that I bought with my first big chunk of money, when I was seventeen. I found myself lovingly placed in my bed the next morning. Night is different here.

Different types of darkness to the darkness here will eliminate humankind from Earth. The maps I look at show that dark eating our places and replacing them with something. Something dark. So very dark.

I have a movie about extinction on in the background because I cannot live in this small space alone. That apocalyptic saga with its heroes and its future lives contains so much more hope than my small room does. Everyone who made the film believed that humankind would continue. I know that the moment I stop writing, the dark will come for me, just as it has come for my friends.

It was no chance that we all knew each other. None. We were a group of writers who love writing an end of things. We wrote in different genres and in different ways and were none of us alike, but we wrote endings, not beginnings. We became the documenters of that end. Darkness finds happiness in that.

I want Skynet and a war with machines. I want tripods and a war with Mars. I want... hope.

All I have is a space that becomes smaller the longer I am in it.

***

After all these days alone, I wondered why we had gas masks. It was as if the smoke I'd travelled through to get here no longer existed. That was not a memory to me. My life was fictional and only these rooms were real.

I put a mask on and pinched it tight over my nose. I took five steps into the dark and found myself... in a compound. Everything was green and pleasant.

It took me a bare few minutes to find another human being. The others were there. My missing writerly friends. They weren't wearing masks, so I took mine off. I stood still in the green glade with its oddly indirect sunlight and breathed deeply, filling my lungs with unexpectedly fresh air.

"I thought you were dead." My ex welcomed me in the style that ensures he will always be my ex.

"Welcome to the zoo," said one of the others.

"We have no idea why we're here," said Sheryl, with no cheer in her voice. I've known Sheryl for twenty years. She is not someone who seeks unhappiness.

I asked them if they'd looked at the maps and...

"That was boring." Guess who said that? "I played computer games."

"Wait," said Sheryl. "Tell us about them."

"They document the destruction of humanity. I don't think it was a computer game."

"Come and look here." Sheryl pulled me through the green, past garden chairs and a fountain. We came to an abrupt stop. We stood next to a wall. It swirled in greens and golds and was completely opaque. I couldn't tell if it was some sort of liquid or some sort of solid, but it entranced me. "I know that feeling," said Sheryl. "I stared at it for hours. You can do that later, if you still want. Me, I want to get away from the wall, so let's get this over with. I hate this wall." She took a deep breath and said, "Brace yourself."

Sheryl reached out and touched the wall. An area about the size of an adult human cleared. She moved her finger along until the transparent area grew large enough to step through. I reached to touch it and it was glass. Liquid glass. It was impenetrable and yet it flowed around my fingers.

With my hand still reached out, and my index finger trying to understand the strange sensation of the material, I saw a finger touching mine. Or was it a claw? A claw with joints and a nail and... It was a claw. I followed the claw with my eyes and discovered a giant lizard, with yellow frills around its head. Its eyes were like ours, until I looked more closely. They were facetted. The lizard's eyes twirled and sparkled at me like a blue-green kaleidoscope. I withdrew my hand in a hurry.

Then I stared.

On the other side of the wall we were being gawped at by strange creatures. Not just a claw. A dozen strange things. They were all lizards. The one with the yellow frills was the smallest. Every one of them looked at us with those facetted, twirling eyes. It was... discomfiting.

"We're in a zoo," I said, stupidly.

"We *are* the zoo."

"I want to go back to my lounge room." It suddenly felt much safer.

"You have to go home to eat. They don't let any of the food through the dark. We can't find any reason for this at all, so we think, maybe, it's local custom."

"The dark doesn't go away?"

"The masks will replenish themselves, just like the damn food does. We get one trip out here a day. It can be as long as we like." That was when I realised just how warped my timesense had become. Sheryl spoke as if she had been there for weeks. For me, it was only days.

I'm a part of the Human section of a zoo. I have no idea where the zoo is. The science of it defeats all of us. I was the only one able to handle the maps showing us the way the world ends, but eventually everyone agreed that the end of Earth was twenty years away.

Our media is back. The internet is ours as long as we read it and don't try answering anyone. This annoys my ex who keeps wanting to argue with everyone who annoys him. That used to entertain me. Now I tell him, "Get over it."

We get to write about home dying. We're the zoo and we're witnesses. That means we'll be here for twenty years, at least.

Everything we write appears as script on those fancy walls. This. This is what you're reading now. I pretend I'm writing to humans but honestly, I don't know who you are and why you would want to read it. Your eyes make me dizzy.

If we write a lot then people admire the script and not us. By 'people' I mean aliens. You.

Honestly, twenty years in the future is completely fictional when we're stuck in our little rooms and our pretty green garden. If I were writing it as a story, I'd wonder where the impetus came from to get us out and return us home. I'd put in having a Babel fish and magically learning alien lingo.

In reality, we're in a perpetual garden party where we each storm out or sulk or drift out and go solitaire. They're watching us, whatever creatures these be, for Sheryl tried suicide. She was the first, but not the last. None of us have succeeded.

I don't know if Earth has survived or if fire and darkness ate everyone, but we are very popular. There are always gawkers. We write about them sometimes, but it's hard to write about strange creatures when the wall becomes opaque so very quickly. The lizards don't want us to look out, or make polite conversation. I think they're scared of us, but my ex thinks they think we're just monkeys. Monkeys who eat tinned food. I hate tinned food.

I can't tell you what I really think, but if you can read between the lines, ask how long our voyage here took and why we're kept so much alone. I do wonder what happened when these aliens tried to bring their apocalypse to Earth. I can't tell you, because you're an alien reading my writing on the wall.

I can dream it. You can't read my dreams, can you?

Wollemi Dreaming

Jason Nahrung

The theme of this anthology struck a spark, and it landed in tinder: images of the Black Summer bushfires still burning at the time this story was written and the incredible efforts of specialist firefighters in protecting the unique Wollemi pine stand in New South Wales; climate change; and crimes against our First Nations peoples. It's not so hard to imagine the hubris of the wealthy privileged preying on the desperate to destroy part of our natural world that others risked their lives to save. But this story lets nature defend itself.

Jason Nahrung

Wollemi Dreaming
by
Jason Nahrung

The guard gives a casual salute, two fingers together flicking from his forehead under the brim of his battered Akubra as they drive out the gate. No questions when you're leaving; plenty when you're coming back, but they've got passes. All good. The client's taken care of it and Jimmy feels the familiar surge of joy as they leave the enclave, the sky opening up above the hazy line of blue-green mountains to the west.

The buggy chews up the broken freeway, through the ruins of the burbs, tyres crunching over rubble. Its cells scrape power from the low morning sun; the buggy's shadow stretches long in front of them, looking like some kind of mutated bug with its bulbous tyres and the skeletal roll cage boggling with spotlights. There's smoke to the north and a few tendrils rising lazily from the mountains in front.

'That gonna be a prob, old man?' Sev shouts over the whir and rattle of the buggy.

Jimmy shakes his head. 'Been plenty through where we're headin'.

'You sure they're still there, then?'

'I seen a report, back in the burnin' times. Said they'd saved 'em.'

'If they're such a big secret, how come you know where they are?'

'I told ya, we went there plenny before the Crunch. Summer holidays, campin', all that stuff. Weren't allowed near 'em but we knew they were there. Kinda.'

'I dunno,' Sev says, doubt penetrating the dust-caked mask that covers his face.

'At least we're on the hunt,' Jimmy says, glad to be rid of the enclave stench of rotting trash and manure. 'Better than shovellin' shit into bean fields, eh.'

'It's just... Waddo said there was meant to be a wombat or two down south around—'

'Just forget about the wombats, OK? We find these pines, we're sorted.'

'But, trees, Jimmy? Who wants trees?'

'He's some kind of hydroponic millionaire, from Tassie, I think. I only spoke to his agent, like, down at Queenie's. But hey, as long as the money's good. And it is. Very bloody good. Better than we'd get for a wombat. And a lot less hassle, too.'

They travel quietly after that, tired of shouting through the masks. Sev drives, Jimmy rides shotgun with the rifle loose in his gnarled, melanoma-scarred hands as they wind through the blackened outer burbs, the houses little more than twisted corrugated iron and bits of wall. Waste of time stopping, they've been picked clean ages ago, and only crows hunt there now, though who knows what they find to eat. One thing Jimmy's learned–there's always someone around to profit from others' mistakes. Ash rises under the tyres and Jimmy checks his mask seal, can smell the acrid charcoal even after all these years.

They pass another enclave, its ramshackle walls glittering with solar panels and spiked with jury-rigged turbines turning lazily in the torpid air. Sev steers them well clear in case someone wants a pot shot; Jimmy can feel the scopes watching as they follow the main road west. They breathe easier once they reach paddocks with fence posts blackened like used match sticks, lines of rusty barbed wire like the spines of giant snakes coiled uselessly between them. Power poles burned off at ground level, still suspended by the wires from those left intact on either side. Capricious, fire. Takes one, leaves two; Russian roulette with wind for a hammer, blowing things away at random. A matter of if, not when.

Into the foothills and the trees are black skeletons, bare limbs stabbing the sky like they're praying for rain, way too late, and the ground littered with those given up, just laid down to rot. There's a splash of green leaf here and there, tough buggers this lot, but it's pretty desolate and Sev ramps up the tunes on their dented stereo as he steers up the narrow road, dodging branches and washouts and rockslips.

'You check the weather?' he shouts.

As if Jimmy wouldn't. As if Sev hasn't. First thing anyone does. Chance of rain? UV level? Dust storm? Fire?

Jimmy shoots him a glance. Not like Sev to be nervous on a run. 'It's all good.'

'Wouldn't wanna get stuck up here in a flash flood or somethin'.'

'No chance.'

This blasted landscape still amazes him, how quickly things changed. The city caught between the hungry sea and the driving dust and the constant threat of fires. The sparkling capital now a hovel, hanging on for dear life at the edge of the continent. Makes him glad he and his missus didn't have a kid. She'd gone troppo. Antarctica and tundra and feedback loops and tipping points. Changing the house and the way they did things, protesting, having panic attacks over carbon footprints. Until the only footprints were hers, going out the door, to achieve who knew what.

The sun drives into Jimmy's shoulders, the buggy's battery lapping it up. Wishes he could plug himself into it, drain some of this heat. Too soon for a swig of water. They've got the buggy loaded but need room for seedlings; it's a real balancing act.

They camp the night off the road. Jimmy doesn't sleep much, thanks to a curlew that won't shut up. Its cry sounds like a lost person calling coo-ee. Sev snores through, tells him in the morning that he must've been dreaming. What would a curlew be doing out here, in the ash lands?

The next day is more of the same, pushing through mountain tracks, trying to follow the client's rumpled map that supplements Jimmy's faded memory. Backtracking if they can't force a way through, an eye on the battery as the humped peaks block the direct sun.

'Too bad the client didn't spring for new cells and a battery,' Sev says as they grind past a dry lake.

'Least of our worries once we get the score,' Jimmy says, distracted, wondering if that was the weir he and his old man used to fish at, back in the day. The map is all squiggles, like looking at a can of worms, and he can't shake the sound of trickling water, the plop of a baited line hitting the water.

They spend the night on top of a ridge, in a clear space in a former camp ground, the ground a mottled grey under the sparse tufts of spiky grass making a comeback. The scrub around them is thick with regrowth speared by naked trunks showing signs of life in moss and clusters of green leaves. Dinner's a stew of beans and vegies that leaves Jimmy's stomach rumbling, but that's nothing new. There's cracking in the scrub once the sun's gone down, possums and such he supposes, whatever's been able to find enough tucker out here to live on, but to Jimmy the rustling is too close to the crackle of tinder catching fire, the popping of sap.

Come sun-up, Jimmy's knackered, eyes gritty from lack of sleep, and Sev's in a mood; they've used their tiny ration of milk and are down to what passes for black tea, traded with a caravan from the north. Says he couldn't shake the idea of someone in the trees watching him, but when he went to check it out, it was just knot holes in a sapling. Beady, he says; he hacked them out with his survival knife. Maybe it's the smell of smoke that's got to him. Stronger this morning and there's a haze in the west and another to the north, a distant pincer threat they need to keep an eye on as they head northwest, but it's not so bad that they need their battered masks.

'How much further?' Sev asks, reminding Jimmy of his little brother and the gangrene stench that always follows, and he shakes himself free of it. Nah, just as well he hadn't had a kid. He doesn't think too hard about Sev, how he's about the right age, if him and his missus had got around to it.

Sev seems relieved when Jimmy tells him today sometime, depending on the road. He tips the dregs of his tea on the embers of the fire and scuffs dirt over it.

'Let's do it, then.'

Jimmy doesn't argue with him about the tea. It's the last of it, and they've reused the leaves till they're tasteless. He thinks about the pay day at the end of this and all the tea that he can drink. Maybe even coffee. Now that'd be something. They pack quickly.

They pull up in the early afternoon. They've followed a back road as far as they can down into a valley, but fallen trees have blocked it and it's too big a job to clear and the ground's too rough to even think about trying to go around. They pause, drinking in the sight. If the area has ever burned, there's no sign, and the trees are tall, thrusting up out of a tangle of saplings and clawing vines. The air is fresh, no sign of ash, so cool on Jimmy's flushed face.

'Unreal,' Sev says. 'You reckon we could live here?'

'On what?' Jimmy thumps the gum tree that has straddled the road, knocking fungus from its crumbling bark. 'Shank's pony it is, then.'

Sev stares at the forest that chokes the hillsides stretching up on either side of them. 'How we gonna carry the pines?' There's the start of an annoying whine in his tone that Jimmy knows too well.

'We just need a half dozen little ones. We got the packs.' Although the idea doesn't impress him, his knees twinging with the thought.

Sev shrugs into the tanks; Jimmy's got the rucksack that holds what they need for the trees. The straps bite into his shoulders, back muscles protesting already, sweat soaking his spine. The rifle, slung awkwardly over a shoulder, bumps against the machete at his hip, and the canteen sloshes with every step.

'We're close,' he tells Sev as the young fella slumps under the weight of gear and tanks, the nozzle tied to the side. 'I saw it on the telly. They were saying how the mountain burned but they'd saved the valley. These pine trees, old as dinosaurs. Of all the things worth saving, hey. Shit hit the fan about that, but I guess once the Crunch smashed everything, no one gave a damn. Too busy scrappin' over what was left, eh.'

'Why would anyone want 'em now?'

'Beats me. All I know is he wants at least six, and no else can have any.'

Sev mulls that and for a moment, Jimmy thinks he's gonna burr up. Then Sev shakes his head. 'Let's just get 'em and get outta here. Place gives me the willies.'

They follow a path beside a dry gully, the scrub pushing in on both sides, grasping at their sleeves and trousers, and the bush so quiet, their footsteps and breaths seem like an assault. Trees stripe the path with shadows, and in places they see kangaroo shit and the occasional marker post that matches the crinkled park map the client gave them. No birds though. Maybe that's what's got them both spooked. The quiet. Not a parrot, not a magpie, no eagle wheeling on a thermal. But then, Sev wouldn't know any different. He's never seen lorikeets blazing through the branches, been laughed at by a kookaburra. Best he's encountered is the ibis and the crows, picking on their leftovers, and the occasional cockatoo attack on the paddocks the enclave has carved out of parks and vacant lots.

They reach a pond and race each other to the beach-like bank littered with dry leaves and stones. The water's so clear, they can see the bottom.

Sev pauses, his knees muddy, cupped hands dripping near his hairy chin, and his grin dries up. 'You reckon it's safe?'

'Nothin' up here, go for it.'

They slurp it up, refill their canteens.

'Like mother's milk,' Sev says. 'Better than beer.'

'Steady on,' and they laugh.

Then Sev freezes, staring across the pond to the ferny bank on the other side.

'What's that—who's that?'

Jimmy looks up, about to thump his paranoid mate for scaring him cold, but then he sees her too.

A girl, dark against the shadows of the cycads, almost a tree herself. Late teens, maybe twenty.

The rifle is back where he shrugged off the pack, a couple of feet away.

'It's okay,' Sev says. 'We won't hurt ya.'

'No,' she says.

'What does that mean?'

'I dunno,' Jimmy says, then asks her, 'What are you doin' here?'

'I live here.' She steps out into a clear spot. She's wearing shorts, singlet and sneakers. 'What are you doing here?'

'She's a bit of all right,' Sev says.

'Enough of that. We're here for the trees, that's it.' Then to the woman: 'Are you here by yourself? It isn't safe.'

'Safer here than anywhere else.'

'Well, I guess it hasn't burned.' He feels the presence of the tanks sitting next to his pack like a malignant throb, itching like melanoma.

'Why are *you* here?' she asks.

'We're looking for the pines. You know the ones?'

'The grove is taboo. You can't go there.'

'Well, we kind of have to. It'd speed things up if you could tell us where exactly it is.'

She frowns, then repeats, 'It's taboo.'

'You here by yourself? How do you manage?'

'My mother's here. My whole family.'

'Do you have sisters?' Sev asks. 'Are they all as pretty as you?'

'My brothers are prettier,' and she flashes a smile that dazzles like sunlight on water.

'Very funny,' Sev says.

'We can give you food, medicine,' Jimmy says, the lie coming out slick as oil. 'If you tell us where the trees are.'

'Actually, my mother isn't well. If you can help her, maybe I'll think about it.'

They remount their packs and follow her along the gully. A wallaby thumps through the underbrush. Sev jerks towards the sound, a hand reaching for the nozzle. Jimmy has a flash vision of the wallaby cooking in a hole in the ground, of juice on his chin, of a full belly.

'That's my brother,' the girl says. 'You don't have to worry.'

'Sure,' Sev says, and when she moves on ahead, makes a cuckoo crazy gesture beside his forehead.

Jimmy smiles at him, rolls his eyes, but there's something unsettling about this, and he feels a chill here in the dimness, in this oasis with the chuckle of the creek, water as clear as glass, not a hint of ash anywhere. Amazing. He feels dirty, weighed down by all the dust on his boots and clothes, the sweat that sticks his shirt to his back. He wants to jump into the water but feels it would be a sin, that he isn't worthy. Tears burn in his eyes and he quickly looks away from Sev, as though searching the slopes around them until he regains control.

A little further up the track they reach a humpy of bark and saplings, flashes of blue tarpaulin in the roof and a flap of it covering the door. A fire pit with a billy outside, reminding Jimmy of his family's camping trips, the scent of wood smoke in his clothes and hair, comforting, not a threat like it is now.

'Here,' the girl says, and steps aside, into the shrubs that crowd around the humpy.

Jimmy pulls the tarp aside carefully, as though a snake might lurk on the other side.

There's a thin black woman on a camp bed, blanket up to her chin. Her face is grey and mottled with spots and the sweat shines on her skin. She doesn't seem to see him. He can smell the rank illness, feel it in the dim closeness of the air inside the hut. He backs out, wishing he was wearing his mask, turns towards the girl, asks, 'What's wrong with her? Measles?'

But the girl isn't there.

'Where'd she go?' he asks Sev.

'She was right there. What is it? What's wrong?'

Jimmy walks over to a cycad taller than he is. He hits the fronds with his machete, shakes his head as he pokes around it and its neighbours.

He walks back to the humpy, reefs the canvas aside to ask the old lady what the game is, then stumbles back from the door.

'She's gone too.'

'Who?'

'Take a look.'

The camp bed and the blanket are empty. There's a sack leaking flour, some shrivelled plants in a wooden dish on the floor. But no one's there, just spider webs and dust.

'What's going on?' Jimmy asks, unslinging the rifle, taking comfort in the solid timber of the stock, the weight of it.

There's a loud thunk, axe on wood.

Sev jerks towards the noise. 'What's that?'

They stand side by side. Sev pulls his machete. Jimmy works the bolt to push a round into the chamber.

'Is that a chainsaw now?' Sev asks.

'Wait ... no, it's a bulldozer, somethin' like that.'

'How can that be?'

'I dunno. Maybe someone's after the trees. Shit! Let's get up there. Grab the tanks.'

They load up. The smell of wood smoke clouds around them. Jimmy kicks the fireplace; it's long dead, just dirt and coals and blades of grass poking up through the grey inside the circle of stones.

Jimmy checks the map. 'The pines are up there somewhere. Can't be far.'

They scramble up the slope through the ferns and shrubs. They've barely lost sight of the creek before they're covered in fresh sweat.

The smell of smoke gets heavier as they climb, a blue haze settling around them like a mountain fog as they push past mould-splashed boulders, grass trees, and then pale, smooth trunks of ghost gums. Crows call them names and possums growl in the undergrowth like they're on midnight heat. The noise is a saw cutting into their hearing, grinding on their nerves.

Sev slices at trees, just because he can.

The northerly wind picks up. Trees clatter around them, branch on branch.

'Smell that?' Jimmy says, huffing for breath. 'What is that?' The scent of diesel is choking, the mist swirls like steam; there's a Geiger counter click louder than any cicadas.

'Nothin',' Sev says, eyes wide, nose twitching, and Jimmy thinks he's a bloody liar.

They pause for a swig of water. Sev blows his nose, one finger to his nostril, then the other. The snot shoots out black. Their faces are covered with soot.

'Get your mask,' Jimmy says.

Sev pats at his belt, his kit. 'I don't have it.'

Jimmy can't find his, either. 'Did we leave 'em at the buggy?'

'Dunno. Maybe that girl...'

'Maybe.'

'C'mon, not far now.'

But Sev stands still, sniffing at the smoky air. 'Feel that?'

'Feel what?'

'The wind.'

The trees whip in a hot, dry wind that dries the sweat on Jimmy's forehead. His guts tighten.

'Shit, that's a fire front.'

Ash drifts down, like snow, like he imagines snow to be. The valley fills with a distant roar, like a giant inhaling, and when it blows out...

Sev is obviously thinking the same thing, his eyes wide in his ash-smeared face.

'Could work in our favour,' Jimmy says with a bravado he doesn't feel. He taps the tanks on Sev's back. 'Hide what we're up to.'

'Unless it catches us here.'

'It's comin' from the north. We're goin' the other way. We got time. But yeah, let's not stuff around.'

The wind drives them, gives them a reason to ignore the burn in their legs, in their chests. The ash gets thicker, coats Jimmy's throat; he can feel it clogging his lungs, making breath harder to draw.

'Hear that?' Sev asks, his voice cracking.

'What now?'

'Sounds like screams?'

'Nah, it's that chainsaw again. There must be a team out, tryin' to save the trees. But they don't know about us.'

'Nah, can't be. There aren't any teams no more. Not out here.'

'Just keep walkin'. We gotta find them trees. Or you wanna be a crispy critter?'

Sev stares around, his hands on the nozzle, the tube twisting back to the tanks like a worm.

'Just calm down,' Jimmy tells him. 'We get what we can carry, torch the rest, and we're set.'

'Do we really gotta burn it, Jimmy?'

Jimmy rubs a hand over his sweaty scalp. 'The collector doesn't want no one else to have 'em. I guess it's gonna go up eventually. Everything has.'

'It'll come back, right?'

'Somethin' will. Not this exactly, but somethin'.'

Clouds of smoke block the sun; the north is an orange glow through the canopy, casting them in amber freckled with drifting ash.

Sticks crack in the brush.

Sev jerks from one point to another. 'Who's out there?'

'No one's out there, just relax, can't ya. Hey, I can see somethin'. C'mon.'

They charge through the weird twilight. Jimmy slices a bush away from a sheet of metal, the black script barely readable on the weathered yellow panel. *Biosecurity area. Trespassers will be prosecuted.*

'This is it,' he says. Money could grow on trees. Just ask all those loggers, back in the day.

Excitement powers his tired legs as they push up the hill. They slash bushes out of sheer exuberance. The scrub thins out; tall trees, trunks as thick as bridge pylons, make a kind of grove as they top the incline.

They stop in awe, silence falling as they take in the sight of the trunks leathered like crocodile skin, the clustered needles, the scent of... of freshness. Jimmy thinks of his mother, of the beach, of the first light at the camp site, of dawn breaking through his bedroom window, of roast cooking in the oven. It has been so long since he's eaten roast beef, since he's felt any of these things. Tears well and he swipes them away fiercely.

A crack as loud as thunder shatters the silence; the cool evaporates.

The trees toss like brumbies. Another crack, this time followed by the crunching as the branch smashes its way through its fellows and thumps to the needle carpet. Like a giant's footsteps, getting closer, crack, crack, thump.

'Widowmaker,' Sev says, fear edging his words.

'Don't worry about it. Let's get what we came for.' Jimmy drops his pack. 'Where's ya shovel?'

'Me what?'

'Ya shovel?' Jimmy turns Sev around, flicks the loose strap where the shovel should've been tied to the side of the tanks. He flicks a loose strap, cursing himself for not having noticed. 'How we gonna dig the trees out?'

'You got yours.'

Jimmy wants to unfold it, lock it in place and slap Sev with it.

'All right, then. Keep an eye out. Let's start with that one.'

Sev hits the switch and flame licks at the spout as Jimmy bends over the little pine, a miniature Christmas tree.

The branch comes down, a crack the only warning, the rush of the leaves. Sev is smacked to the ground and hits the trigger, shooting a tongue of flame into the air. It catches a gum tree that goes up like a firework, so hot and quick it takes Jimmy's eyebrows off.

Sev is a flaming, screaming mess flailing under the branch.

The gum seems to bend, the flames leaping as it showers embers.

Jimmy stumbles back, trips, falls, rolls behind one of the pine trees. The flame divides around it, like a crab claw reaching. He scrambles back, driven by the intense heat, and then the ground falls away and he is rolling and thumping, bouncing off tree trunks and boulders, and the flame flares after him. All he can see is red fire and the black and grey of things he thumps into.

He is in the open air, flailing.

Splashes down, goes under.

Comes up spluttering.

Ducks as flames roar overhead, a steam train hissing and sputtering.

He struggles to the bank. The forest writhes, a nightmare of red and black, the air thick with choking smoke. Steam rises from the water; the stench of burnt hair fills his nostrils.

He follows the creek, like a zombie shuffling over the rocks in water that warms and runs the colour of blood in the bushfire twilight. He has lost a boot, his foot sliced on rocks through his threadbare sock. Pain wracks his body. He wishes for the supplies in his pack, no doubt as toasted as Sev by now, back in the grove, but there is a first-aid kit at the buggy, he can dose up, let the car do the work as he back tracks.

He emerges from the valley into the dry browns of the parched forest glowing under the red sky. Every step an agony, one arm hanging as he tries to stop the bones from rubbing together, at the very brink of throwing up or passing out. The heat beams down like an alien's laser and the world is lurid, but there finally is the buggy. He doses up on expired meds and pours water down his throat and over his face, wondering how he can make it the two days or more back to the enclave. The roar of fire fills his ears as twin tongues follow the sides of the valley, and he knows they will converge on him. If he doesn't get moving.

He hits the starter.

Nothing.

The battery's dead, the cells caked in ash and dust, unable to snare any brightness from the ashen glow. How long were they in the valley? Two hours? Three? He slumps in the driver's seat, his chest on fire as though a spear has been rammed into it. The fire descends like a coal train, and all he can see is flame, all he can hear is screams.

OZ is Burning

Firestorm Sounds

Suzanne Newnham

I wrote Firestorm Sounds not just to chronicle my story with extreme hypersensitivity to sounds, but to show thought processes dealing with a chronic medical condition while trying to cope with pain in a world on fire; to create awareness of hidden disability; and be a voice for those unable to express their pain.

Suzanne Newnham

Fire burns. It is hot and reduces fuel to ash and smoke which taints the air we breathe. We are familiar with these symptoms. But there are people who taste color, smell beauty, and feel emotions on their skin. Do we ever think of these alternative reactions to what happens around us? I bought this story because it reminds us that not everyone sees the same fire.

Phyllis Irene Radford

Firestorm Sounds
by
Suzanne Newnham

Midst the chaos of bushfires and evacuations there was another fear, another situation that continually teetered on the brink of being a medical emergency throughout this time and afterwards. It's not a normal medical condition, there's no diagnosis... just 'extreme hypersensitivity to sounds and vibration' causing throat muscles to swell, reducing breathing, increasing fatigue, and exacerbating chronic pain. But it's not just the pain, the continual reactions, as well as some of the medications, plays havoc with my brain. My words slur, bits of words trail, sentences become muddled, and while I have found writing a way to restore cognitive abilities, it takes a lot of effort–too much at times–with no energy left to edit the way I would have done in the past.

Aircraft fly overhead, one to the south-west, another north-west, with barely a few minutes before they fly towards the river for another refill. The fires must be close, too close. Motors whirr, rotor-blades scream but I look into the reddened sky and murmur "thank you" to the courageous men and women and their machines trying to contain the fire-spread. Reaching for an inhaler again to persuade my swelling throat muscles and compromised breathing to settle; my body stings from sounds that aggravate my fragile state of health. More pills are taken, oils and creams to soothe, I know I can get through this–I have to! Another whirr cuts the air as a chopper carrying life-saving water flies overhead, but this time all I can manage is a weak smile. My noise-cancelling headphones clamped to my ears don't shut out the noise and vibration thundering through my body.

Tears well, and I convince myself that they are more to release the pressure building up in my head rather than crying. What use is the latter, I know the sounds will continue and there's no escape.

I focus on notifying family and friends of what's happening with the fires, arrangements, reality, as well as glimmers of hope. A WIFI dongle is my only communication to the outside world–its connection is intermittent but a feeling of joy spreads as I inform others in our living room that another message has been sent to my son. I know he will Facebook post and ring key people to start the network going. The following day there's a window of internet reception once again and I check my son and daughter's postings, questions flood the comment section along with a few private messages. "Do you know about Mossy Point, Surf Beach, Tomakin, other villages and communities close by?"

"What about the retirement home?" asks another. Anxious friends, and friends of friends outside the south coast firestorm, having heard nothing for days, seek information. Not that I can say much but just talking about the evacuation centres, the community spirit of neighbours and strangers looking out for each other seems to reassure even though I can't give specific answers as to whether their relatives and friends are safe.

Another alert, and this time with cars laden, elderly family and I depart for an evacuation centre. In the dead of night tripping over the only tuft of grass, albeit dead, in a paddock of dirt I end up in the local hospital Emergency Department. Relieved, the ambulance officers and hospital night staff seem to accept my fear of sounds, and reach for the non-beeping cuff to measure my blood pressure. In the morning, however, the Emergency waiting room fills and my fears are realised when a monitor starts beeping, my throat starts closing and it's mistaken for a panic attack. I manage to get my inhaler from the clear pouch of medicines I carry with me, and with huge difficulty swallow tablets gagging on the water. My husband arrives from 'firewatch' to take me home, and on seeing him I feel sad that he looks tired and stressed but at the same time so relieved that I don't have to worry about my symptoms being misinterpreted anymore.

Sanctuary, a warm cup of tea, and quiet and my shattered body is able to relax. I'm not sure for how long but it felt as though this blissful time seemed too short as my throat starts to seize and I struggle to breathe again. The sound, almost imperceptible through the cloying dense red smoke, signals another firetruck or emergency service vehicle in the distance. As they get closer sirens blare causing pain to rifle through my body, and now with broken bones in my foot and toes there's a new source of sensitive nerves to jangle. The high-pitched squeals and whirring of rotor-blades overhead, together with monotonous low-pitched droning of aircraft become louder and I again resign myself to living a nightmare. Skin sensitive to pressure I surround my body with soft pillows to try and protect it from the firmness of the sofa. I ache to lie down and drift to sleep but lying down has been long forgotten if I still want to breathe. I feel the colour draining from my face.

I'd like to be comforted, for my pain to go away. But who am I to worry others when the unimaginable is happening all around? They can see my distress. Having witnessed my reactions to sounds many times over the past twelve years, I'm aware they feel helpless knowing they're incapable of offering the type of relief I really need.

I try to downplay what's happening but the grey pallor in my face is too obvious. I can't stand because my legs seem to have been replaced by jelly. My spirit flags causing my body to slump as my sense of survival is threatened. The thought of all the sounds which affect me surfaces and I long for the world to cease replacing silent electronics with all manner of beeps, to make phone ringtones that aren't so piercing, and for the plethora of leaf blowers, and other noise producing gardening equipment be banned or at least have silencers fitted. How I wish safety fittings on vehicles don't produce sounds that can be heard through closed windows a block away–no sounds or vibrations of the type that continually set off a breathing and pain reaction. If only... and now this. But I must remain strong, I have to, who am I to want the aircraft to stop flying overhead and dropping its water on the inferno nearby?

I can't control any of what's happening outside, adrenaline's running rife therefore rest is impossible so as in the past I take to writing. It doesn't stop the pain, and I still struggle for air but it's a distraction. Then a thought occurs to me—how would I write in my magazine column about coping with chronic pain and hypersensitivity in extreme conditions? Moreover, how can I write about coping if I can't cope? My thought process gradually changes as I ponder how to not go under when hypersensitivities are being challenged, and for an extended period of time. Now with the bushfires I write notes, I think about strategies and how I can deal better with the sirens, the droning aircraft, the reaction next time. For unfortunately there will be a next time.

It's now been two weeks since fires were on our doorstep and our home is safe. I haven't coped very well, but at least I've survived. Oh no, once again I sense my energy draining, and muscles feel like they're sagging, as my throat starts to close, and I struggle to breathe. Frantic to remember what to do, and quickly, I find my inhaler and take a couple of puffs but obviously not quick enough as the tablets feel stuck. It seems to take ages for the tablets to release and for air to feel as though it was making an effort to reach my lungs. What next? I think-talk to myself trying to reduce the 'fight and flight' response from flooding my body with even more of the chemicals that I react to–I can't use an Epipen which is the usual device to use with an allergic reaction as it will only inject more of what my body is fighting against–I'm exhausted, skin stinging with pain racing through me finding new areas to stab. Sitting with my head back to allow an easier passage for air and the immediate urgency dissipating, I'm aware of a barely perceptible but unmistakable sound increasing to a roar as a water-bombing aircraft flies overhead. Obviously, the fires are still close.

As the sound of the aircraft fades into the distance, I eventually manage to bring another struggle for air and acute flare-up of chronic pain under better control. In the living room the television is on and I hear a news presenter talking about the heavy rains and hoping it brings an end to the fires, and the drought, along the east coast. Rain dances must have been successful, I whisper to the air. However, my satisfied grin doesn't remain for long when the news item finishes with "And the township of Moruya is now on flood alert"

Red Sky, Blue Dreams

Jack Dann

"Red Sky Blue Dreams" came to me in an almost hallucinatory form, perhaps because it resonated with an unretouched photo I took a few days ago at the farm in South Gippsland

Jack Dann 10 January 2020
Windhover Farm,
Victoria, Australia

OZ is Burning

.

Red Sky, Blue Dreams
by
Jack Dann

The sky is burning coals and curling clouds,
Curling red weather, fire weather

Fire skies, fire thunder and fire
Water poisoned with ash

Tank water smelling of politics,
Politicians smelling of denial

Remember the coal you brought
To Parliament, Mr. Prime Minister?

Did you take it to Hawaii?
Or is it in a dark drawer

In a red-lit parlour?
Red coals now the color of our lives

And we just the hot, charred figures
Cavorting in the burning night

In a diorama that was once a country
Now black desiccations of flora of fauna

Scattered in the red Night

OZ is Burning

A billion creatures dead in red

Destroyed like homes
And dreams and heroes

And you and me under our red sky
A roaring red sky raining fire and

Politicians' ashen denials
While we yet dream blue dreams of blue skies
And cumulus bright-cloud futures for this
Sun baked burning hell of a Lucky Country.

Infestation

Paula Boer

I was inspired to write this story as not only were all 500 acres of my property burnt during the January 2020 bushfires, but as a migrant to Australia, I have been horrified by the impact that settlement since 1788 has had on native flora and fauna. Europeans brought with them not only pests and diseases, but ignorance and arrogance over the indigenous people's way of life. Not much has changed in the 200+ years since.

Paula Boer

Infestation
by
Paula Boer

Antipodes groans, the weight of wisdom heavy in her bones, her great age measured by her far location on the planet. Calved by Gondwana before the extinction of dinosaurs, she drifts across the seas, her head breathing in the tropics, her toes dabbling in the frigid waters of the southern ocean. Her tail lies partially submerged to the east, rising and falling in islands as eons pass.

For millennia she has slumbered, her changing rhythms barely noticeable by the life she succours, all of it in balance, flora and fauna, predator and prey, wet season and dry. She has no desire to rise or fall, to join her continental cousins in their upheavals.

Until, over the horizon, ships sail from the far side of the earth, invading her shores, bringing plagues of greed and righteousness. Swarms of parasites plunder her reserves of gold and diamonds, tin and copper. Open wounds fester on her torn rump, raw gashes exposing long dead forests, pipes drilling down to suck out her blood. Nightmares torment her.

She awakes, eyes glazed in pain, unaware of what has caused the change. She studies her surface, shocked at what she sees. No longer sleek and well cared for, her bones protrude, and sores cover her skin. Horror pierces her core. She jolts fully alert. Who dares do this to her? She questions the weather, but he says he is not to blame. She asks the sun and moon, but they deny all knowledge of what ails her. Finally, after seeking answers far and near, an ancient whale answers her. 'Look closer to home. You are infested.'

She observes herself, unbelieving as the truth is revealed. Enough! No more can she permit the pulping and planking of her cloak of trees. No more can she allow the ploughing and pollution of her soils. No more can she accept the damming and destruction of her waters.

She breathes in deeply, sucking the moisture from the air, exposing her hide to the ferocious sun. Plants wither and animals die of thirst. Marshes and swamps transform to deserts. Birds plummet from the sky, exhausted and dehydrated. The air ripples with heat, shimmering mirages teasing inhabitants to wander to their deaths.

The parasites build stronger homes, locking themselves away from contact with her, congregated together in colonies formed of her bones. They breed and multiply, exporting her worth in return for technology that removes them further from her embrace. They introduce monocultures and alien species, overrunning her native inhabitants and continuing the rape of her gifts.

Her droughts continue, but still the parasites prevail. She shivers her tail, breaking open her wounds, her ichor pouring forth in vast plumes of lava and steam. The seas rise and pound her sides, washing away those too wary to keep away. The surrounding ocean warms in response, upsetting the fragile balance of life below the surface, removing the shallow nurseries for fish and crumbling the deep haunts of gargantuan marine life.

Nothing deters the parasites, not lack of food nor absence of fresh water, not rattling her bones nor flapping her invisible wings. A harsher deterrent is required.

Antipodes huffs out her anger and ignites the tinder of her desiccated flesh, screaming in agony as cleansing flames and smothering smoke destroy all life they envelop. Black stumps point accusingly at each other, crashing down in charcoal lumps. Burning leaves pirouette ahead of the firestorm, igniting unburnt areas. Flames converge and mingle in spiralling tornadoes. The roaring conflagration races hither and thither, indiscriminate in its terror.

The bacteria and fungi that provide Antipodes with nutrients; the myriad insects that pollinate her flowers; the tiny scuttling mammals and reptiles that keep them in check; the herbivores that graze grasslands or nibble leaves high in the forests; the monotremes and marsupials; the bats and birds and snakes and lizards; all become cinders.

The destruction she has caused breaks Antipodes' heart. Icy tears hail down her sides, washing ash and debris into her waterways, clogging flows and suffocating fish. She heaves with sorrow until only the pain remains. No laughing kookaburras welcome the morning, no currawongs call out warnings, no lyrebirds mimic their neighbours. Regret washes through Antipodes like the fire ravaged her surface.

She remembers the great storms she inhaled to bring the drought. Choking back her agony, she draws the clouds into her chest. Moisture swirls and builds until she can no longer contain it, rushing out of every pore, drenching her burnt skin, flooding every crevice and crease. Dry creek beds froth and foam, streams become rivers, billabongs overflow. On and on the torrent continues, washing away all the impurities with her memories.

The outflow ceases. She holds her breath in anticipation. Slowly, steadily, life returns. First a fungal growth coats her skin, breaking down minerals for the plants to follow. Buds erupt from branches and trunks, shoot up from tubers and rhizomes. An insect buzzes, looking for nectar. A frog croaks, seeking a mate. A cockatoo screeches overhead. Soon the air is enriched with noise and fragrant from damp soil and wet grass.

Antipodes sighs with relief. Purged, razed, and scrubbed, she swells with hope. She lets her weary head droop back to the ocean, her chest rising and falling in time with the seasons. Content, she falls asleep once more.

But not all was scoured away. The parasites persist.

Antipodes' nightmares return.

Dire Insurance

Jared Kavanagh

I worked in insurance once. (Once was enough.) I was inspired by that experience to write a story which looks at how there can be lighter moments, even during the most unpleasant times.

Jared Kavanagh

OZ is Burning

Dire Insurance
by
Jared Kavanagh

Sudden termites will ruin anyone's morning.

Ned went to open the cupboard to get his breakfast cereal. When he pulled the handle, the entire door came off. He barely managed to stop the door from falling on his head.

He balanced the door against the kitchen wall. Where the hinges had been attached, he saw two tiny whitish heads poking out of holes in the timber. They both vanished back inside as he approached.

"White ants?" he murmured.

Ned started tapping on a few other doors and walls. Most of them sounded hollow. When he knocked on one wall near the front door, his hand punched a hole in the wall. Most of the timber surrounding the hole had been eaten until only narrow edges remained. A few termites scurried further inside the wall here, too.

"Jesus, they've infested the whole house," he said.

He retrieved his phone, searched for pest control companies, and called the first one on the list. They promised to be there within the hour.

Ned prepared a quick breakfast while he waited. Cornflakes, milk and orange juice were unexciting at the best of times; now, he barely tasted them. He found himself checking the time every couple of minutes.

Fifty-eight minutes later—Ned checked the time on his phone again, just to be sure—a white and yellow van drove through his front gate and stopped outside the door.

"Must've got here earlier and waited down the street," Ned said. Their timing was too precise for him to believe otherwise.

He stepped outside to welcome the pest inspectors. In turn, the smell of smoke greeted him, stronger than yesterday. According to last night's news, the bushfires near town were still burning vigorously. So long as the wind kept blowing from the east, though, the fires should pass by harmlessly.

Two men got out the van, both wearing yellow overalls. One went around to the back and started pulling out equipment, while the other came up to the front door.

"I'm Ollie. Want to show me the problem?"

Ned pointed to the nearby hole in the wall. "White ants. The damned things have eaten through the walls."

"Termites, mate," the pest inspector said. "They're not ants. They're descended from cockroaches. Which explains a lot, really. Where else have you seen them?"

Ned led the inspector to the detached door, then pointed out the other places which had sounded hollow.

"Looks like you've got a plague of 'em, mate. We'll check everything, let you know where they all are."

Both men went to work, systematically examining every wall and floorboard. Ollie used a machine which he said emitted ultrasound, to see termite damage without needing to open walls. He smiled whenever he found more of the little pests.

Ned tugged at his hair every time Ollie smiled, until he smacked his fist into his open palm and stalked out of the house. It was leave or thump a fist into the inspector's odious grin.

Outside, the stench of smoke still hung in the air, as it had for days. This summer had been devastating for fires. Still, better to breathe a little smoke in the outside air than stay inside and have smoke come from his ears in frustration at the termite problem.

The inspectors reappeared briefly to ask how best to get into the roof and under the house. Ned showed them, then went back outside.

Eventually, Ollie reappeared. "We've inspected everything we could reach. I'm afraid the damage is, well, everywhere."

"Why didn't I see anything earlier?"

"Termites eat timber from the inside out, leaving a narrow skin. Hard to spot unless you're doing a full inspection. It's obvious under the house, but I suppose you never go there."

"Haven't needed to."

Ollie said, "Fixing this will be a big job. Massive, really. The termites even ate their way up into the legs of the dining table. Guess you haven't moved it in a while."

"I don't use that table," Ned said. Not since his wife passed on. "What will the repairs involve?"

"To be frank, mate, things are so bad I think you'll need to knock down the whole house and rebuild. The little buggers have got into floorboards, timber walls, roof boards, everything. You're lucky this place is only single-storey, or it'd have fallen down already."

"Is there anything you can do?"

"We can kill the ones that are here, sure. But honestly, mate, you'd be wasting your money. The damage is done. You need to clear out of here and demolish it."

Ned took a couple of deep breaths. "Thanks for telling me." He paid Ollie for the inspection, and the van drove off. The breeze picked up, carrying a stronger stink of smoke, but he put it out of his mind and went back inside.

He tiptoed through the house, trying to keep his footfalls soft. He found his home insurance policy, then went into the lounge room. He reached his favourite reclining chair, and shifted it around a few times to make sure it wouldn't collapse through the floor under him before he settled into it.

He called his insurance company. An automated voice greeted him, and made him navigate through a half-dozen menus and press a lot of buttons. Eventually the voice said, "All of our customer service representatives are currently assisting other callers. Your call is important to us. Please remain on hold until one of our representatives is available to assist you. Your estimated hold time will be between one hundred and nineteen and one hundred and thirty-five minutes."

Ned waited. And waited, and waited. The same automated voice regularly assured him that, despite all appearances, his call was important to them. Between those reassurances, the line played music which sounded as if it had been composed by a frog with a sore throat.

Eventually, he reached a genuine human voice. "My name is Madeleine. How can I help you?"

"I have some-"

"Sorry, sir. I just need to verify your identity first."

Ned had to give his full name, address, date of birth, policy number, and value of his last premium. After giving all of that, he said, "Would you like my shoe size as well?"

"I don't have that on file. What did you want to report?"

"Termite damage. My house is infested with them. I need to get it fixed. It may have to be rebuilt."

"I'm sorry, sir, but you're not insured against termite damage."

"What? I'm fully insured."

She said, "Unfortunately, termites are your responsibility, not your insurer. You aren't covered."

"I have comprehensive home insurance. I've always had comprehensive insurance. I know how important it is to be insured. Full replacement coverage, it says here."

"For insurable events, yes, sir. Not for termites or other pests."

"Ridiculous! I've insured myself against everything. Floods. Fires. Public liability. Faulty electrical writing. Malicious damage by guests. Everything."

"Can I place you on hold for a moment, sir, while I bring up a copy of your policy?"

"If you must."

Several more minutes of clogged-throat frog music blared at him until she returned to the line. "If you check clause 139, exclusions, subclause z, you'll see that vermin damage is excluded."

Ned flipped through pages of small print before he reached the relevant clause. Vermin were indeed excluded. "How is that fair?"

"Insurance is to cover sudden, unforeseeable events, sir. Termite damage is not sudden, it emerges gradually."

"I suddenly discovered them!"

"Pest inspections are a homeowner's responsibility, sir. You should have been checking for them earlier."

"I should have gone with a better insurer."

"You'll find that pest damage is excluded from most insurance coverage, sir."

Ned silently counted to ten before speaking aloud. "So I'm stuck with it?"

"Repairs are your responsibility, yes, sir."

"My whole house has to be rebuilt, probably. I'm retired. How am I meant to pay for that?"

"I'm sorry to hear about your problem," she said, sounding singularly unsympathetic.

"Have a good day, then. I won't be," Ned said, and hung up.

A moment later, his phone started ringing again. He ignored it. Why let the worthless insurers waste more of his time justifying why they weren't paying him?

The phone rang out, then almost immediately started ringing once more. Again, he ignored it until it rang out.

Only when the phone called a third time did he look at the caller's name. It was his son Mick. "Hey, son."

"Dad! Where are you?"

"At home."

"I've been trying to reach you for two hours. Haven't you been watching the news?"

"Been busy with something. What's so urgent?"

"Bushfires! The fire front has changed direction and is heading straight for you. The firies have said the whole town needs to evacuate now."

"Way to make a bad day worse," Ned muttered. "Can you get over here?"

"I'll try, dad. Depends whether they've closed the roads to incoming traffic. Pack some essentials."

Ned spent the next few minutes hurriedly throwing what he could pack into suitcases: clothes, toiletries, computer, photo albums, and some other treasured memorabilia. That done, he waited just inside the front door. Smoke had started to thicken in the southern sky when Mick finally arrived.

"Let's go!" his son said, and hurried to load the suitcases into the boot.

***

Two days passed while Ned stayed at his son's house. Two days full of alarming media reports which made it sound as if every town in a fifty-kilometre radius had been obliterated. One day of smoke so thick it made midday seem like twilight. Another day following where the smoke gradually eased but could still be smelt even when doors and windows were kept completely closed.

The day after, evacuated residents were permitted to return. Mick drove Ned back through a landscape which had been transformed into something almost unrecognisable. Trees had been reduced to charred trunks, with leaves and smaller branches burned away. The undergrowth and most of the grass had been obliterated, replaced by ash and cinders.

As they drew near to Ned's home, they passed the ruins of houses. Some had been burned out entirely, while others had a few brick walls left standing forlornly amidst desolation. A few houses were intact, either from good fortune or from owners who had risked death to stay and defeat the flames that threatened their homes.

They rounded the final corner to what should have been Ned's house. The bricks of the chimney still stood, rising in solitary splendour in an otherwise barren field of ash.

Ned burst out laughing; he could not stop himself.

Mick stared at him. "Have you gone crazy, dad? Your home is burned to the ground, and you're laughing."

Ned's chuckles gradually faded. "Because, son, my house isn't insured to be rebuilt from termite damage. But it's sure as hell insured to be rebuilt from a bushfire."

The Divorce

Donna J. W. Munro

This is a story that makes sense when you look at Earth as person, and many of these stories do.

Phyllis Irene Radford

The Divorce
by
Donna J. W. Munro

Martin straightened the papers the boss, Mr. Green, wanted his estranged partner to sign.

"She can be quite charming," Mr. Green said. His high-backed executive chair spun away from him toward the window and its expansive view of, well—everything. "Beautiful too, but stubborn. Set in her ways."

The chair swung around and he stood, straight as a beam, Armani suit nearly gleaming with splendid perfection in the wash of the blue, day lamps glowing in the recessed cans scattered across the high, white ceiling. The glass desk and the gray walled expanse of the boss' office vibrated the power, the casual control he held over, well—everything.

"Just get her to sign them. Take a pen with you."

Mr. Green pulled his own silver, limited-edition, collectors pen, a gift from the shareholders, from his pocket and passed it to him with a smile. Martin reached out a shaking hand and took the pen, glad when his hand returned to his side, out of the reach of the lord of all that walked. In the window behind Green's perfectly coiffed head, the many creatures of the earth wandered, flashed in second long snaps of video life across the technicolor surface, though more often than not, the focus remained on man. Man driving. Man flying. Man drilling. Man jogging along black tar paths through neighborhoods made of neat yards, ornamental pears trees in green rows, and houses that sprouted up: two stories, three car garages, peaked roofs with asphalt shingles.

"Man," Mr. Green said, gaze following Martin's to watch the chaos of the creatures he ruled. "Who knew such a weakling creature, an afterthought really, would come to be my most valuable asset? She laughed at me when I put a man up in the branches of her trees. Then she felt sorry for it. Begged me to teach it some skills. Give it some tools to survive. Now look at them. Ready to conquer the stars."

The window fixed on rockets spewing clouds from their tails, flying faster than Martin had ever seen. And he'd see some flying.

"That's where the shareholders want us and that's where the real wealth is. Just imagine, all that open space. All the places to claim."

"Places without her." Martin regretted the words, but once spoken, words had wings.

Mr. Green turned and glared, baring his teeth at Martin, but the anger passed, and he chuckled. "I guess so, old friend. Without her... bullshit rules."

The other creatures, the four-leggers and flyers and swimmers didn't skim the surface of the window as much. There were fewer, it seemed.

"Go on, Martin. Charm her into signing. Give her what she wants."

***

Martin flew to her, special pen and papers clutched to his chest. Why did she insist on living so far from everything? As far as you could get without coming back is how Mr. Green described it. Martin leaned on a spiny tree in the middle of a weedy copse, so far from where he'd been, he couldn't see any of the blocky building ranges of the city, only the gentle purples and blues of hills hugging the clutched knees of the mountains they sat with. Martin remembered how Mr. Green used to find her himself, kneel before her and clutch her knees, begging for forgiveness. He wasn't a constant creature. His eye wandered.

But he always used to return to her.

At least once a year.

Love brought him back at first.

Then the itch only she could scratch.

Then her power.

Then he stopped coming all together.

Martin remembered how the days they met up, before all of this business and shareholder bullshit, meant weeks of celebration, of lovemaking and breath stained with wine. How the lady smiled at all of them.

She barely noticed them now, if only to scowl her disapproval.

"Lady?" Martin called. The voice he'd been given so long ago, the beautiful song lay in his throat, stretched. He tried again. "Lady?"

The field lay silent, not even breathing the wind that he'd felt as he flew.

She'd never respond. Not to his new voice. He cleared his throat with a grunt. The first notes that came warbled, tuneless across his beak. He'd forgotten how to sing. The gray suit and tightly laced shoes crushed him in their grip, dampened him like a wall of fog holds sound only for itself.

Mr. Green wanted him to find her, coax her out with pretty promises so like jewels when Mr. Green gave them, now sat as ashes on Martin's tongue, streaking it with the black cowl of dead song.

He growled then. He knew how to sing. She'd made him to sing.

So deep from within, the stretched note bunched and leaped until it rang forth, a song he'd been born to sing, "Mother!"

"Mother!" He sang it, stepping out of the tight black shoes, stuffing off the gray poly fabric and letting his feathers shine.

"Martin," the tree whispered, only it wasn't a tree. It was mother. Beautiful brown face, glistening lips, eyes dark and kind bleeding with spilled sap, wetting her cheeks. Flowers in her hair decked with the glittering bright of butterfly wings. She stretched a brown arm out for him to land on, clutched him close with her leafy fingers. "Sing again, beautiful child. How I've missed you."

As she caressed him, his silvery feathers bloomed with purple shots of color and he remembered.

"The green man—"

"I know, Martin. He wants me to sign away rights to the humans. All of them. He wants to go with them." She stroked him lightly under his beak. Around them the other wild things gathered in clumps, prey and predator alike, at peace, because here their future would be decided. She'd birthed them all, Martin knew. She and Green together made them. But Green forgot how each of them mattered, not just the tool making, engineering humans and their clever machines. He'd ruled them once. Left mother to garden for them all. Balance, she'd once told him, but that had been gone for so long now.

"What terms?" She asked with a calm that didn't match the shaking of her leaves, the shuddering of her roots, stirring the earth beneath her. Terms. There were always new terms.

"To leave you, to spread out to others."

"On his damned rockets with his hoards of humans?"

Martin nodded and shivered in her grasp. Mother could be quite violent when she forgot herself or when rage took her. He'd seen islands flooded under waves and forests leveled by fires. In her clutch, he curled in on himself, shuddering in fear, waiting for woody fingers to curl in and crush him. Instead, she slumped, loosening her hold. Gave in to the loss of what she thought her life would be, what she wanted for her family.

"My terms, Martin, are that he take them all to the stars. Seed them on any damned world he finds. But he will never come back. Him and his kind."

"They'll need provisions. Resources."

Her bitter bark of a laugh cut the air of the meadow with an edge that cut through his bones.

"They've used most of what we have, haven't they? Blackened fields and fouled rivers. Let them take what they will." Mother's eyes flashed. She pulled Martin close to her lips, so all he could see, his whole vision, stretched from lip to lip and word to word. "They leave now, and we'll survive them, my loves."

She took the papers, but refused Green's silver, special issue pen, instead reaching up with her clawed, twig fingers to dab at the sap running from her eyes, mourning the thing that Green killed within her. She signed the deal with her heart's blood, the quick and sticky sugar that fed the bugs, that fed the birds, that fed the hawk, cat, and coyote. She dusted the green of her leaves across it, sealing it with the food of the rabbits and the squirrels. And as she signed, the rockets split the skies with their white bushy tails.

The divorce final in the last stroking letter of her name—Earth.

Martin chose to stay with her and rebuild.

What would the shareholders want with a bird's song, anyway?

OZ is Burning

Inconvenient Visitors; Or, An Un-Restful Cure

I used to live on Skyline Road, Christmas Hills, the (slightly disguised) setting of this book. My clergyman grandfather stayed at a guesthouse on the road, called Windermere. The area had been burnt out in 1960, and in retrospect it was suicidal for my parents to build a house there. Several years after they died, Skyline Road went up in flames during the Black Saturday firestorm in 2009. I thought of the place when asked to write an Australian riposte to H. G. Wells' *War of the Worlds* for the anthology *Battleground Australis*. His novel is very closely linked to place, which he researched closely then merrily destroyed. I thought of what the Martian ray might do to the Australian bush, on a summer high-wind day. Voila, I had my story.

Lucy Sussex

Inconvenient Visitors; Or, An Un-Restful Cure
by
Lucy Sussex

All sorts come to Hazelmere, we've seen them all. That's what happens when a man of business like me, with an eye for the comforts of life, sees potential in a property. The advertisement in the *Argus* caught my eye first: Guesthouse for sale, Easter Hills. I took the train to Yarraman, hired a horse and rode up through farmland then bush, the trees to either side bowing in the wind. Between the wrought iron gates, I went, up the drive to the house on the hillcrest, seeing stables, croquet pitch, kitchen gardens. It had potential, for what, I did not know, until I was sitting on the shady verandah, with a bottle from a local vineyard uncorked, and a rich fruitcake cut into wedges with my penknife. I gazed over the valley, the river below like a lady's silver belt, the little bush-birds hopping after my crumbs, and I felt something unusual: completely at peace.

What a place for a rest cure! I thought, and that was how I advertised it. A bit of refurbishing, a first-rate cook and soon the customers came flocking for luxurious respite. Look at the visitors' book and see: French Counts to opera singers and even a Princess from Samoa.

We just weren't expecting something so foreign, nor so much trouble. I can't say that I had much inkling. Among the visitors, we had one solitary astronomer. He was a convivial chap, and I took up his suggestion to install a telescope. Never used it, since I keep my eye on business, not the skies.

Some of the guests did, but it meant nothing much, even when the weekly papers in the breakfast room were left open at the astronomy section. Mars to me was only a book donated to our small library by a grateful customer, Mr.

Fraser the phrenologist: *Melbourne and Mars: My Mysterious Life on Two Planets*. A bit of a rum title, I thought. He'd actually written it, too.

Our inconvenient visitors made their arrival after a long and hot period. The dam by the gates was lower than usual, and so was our custom. With the extended days of heat, people tended to linger at the beach, enjoying the bathing huts and donkey rides. I had been hoping for a cool and rainy time, the sort that would draw the trampers and the mushroom fanciers, but holidays neared, and still I mopped my brow with my handkerchief.

What we had at Hazelmere then were an odd company, of whom the following figured: old Colonel Schmidt and his wife; Mr. Mowbray, a journalist, who mostly sat in his room working on a novel of Australian Life; Curate Pentland, afflicted with the nerves; Miss Royce, a lady not in her first youth, whom rumour said had been sent to recover from an unsuitable attachment. Then there were the staff: besides the three maids, myself and my dear wife, who was housekeeper; Job, the ostler, an Australian of the original type; Ah Kee the Gardener, who was Chinese and nicknamed Archy; and Monsieur Didier the chef, as nervy as any of our customers.

I was, I admit, not enjoying the best of days. Breakfast came with yet more relentless sun, followed by a row in the library. I subscribe to the best periodicals and Robertson the bookseller regularly sends a parcel of fashionable novels. Now Colonel Schmidt had mislaid *The Yellow Wave: A Romance of the Asiatic Invasion of Australia*, and intemperately accused Miss Royce of stealing it.

'As if I would read such rubbish!' the lady retorted loudly.

'Rubbish?' shouted the Colonel. Outside the window Archy was watering the geraniums, pretending at being oblivious.

'Yes, rubbish that is all jingo and UnChristianity!' she continued. I frantically scanned the library shelves, for something, anything of the futuristic ilk, even if it was *Melbourne and Mars*. Then I literally put my hand on the solution.

'Perhaps you might like *The Battle of Dorking*, Colonel Schmidt?' I proffered, and next moment regretted it deeply.

Miss Joyce laughed out loud. 'Colonel *Schmidt*, you would prefer a German invasion of England to an Asian invasion of Australia?'

Mrs. Colonel, an anxious little dove, promptly had hysterics. When all the shouting was over, the Schmidts decamped down to the station, driven by Job in the trap. Archy, now weeding near the gate, raised his conical hat to them. I was having deep suspicions about the fate of *The Yellow Wave*.

The only person unaffected by the row was the journalist Mowbray, who witnessed the disturbance without pausing in his breakfast.

'Might have been worse,' he said. 'You could have offered him *The Coming Terror*, that's written by a genuine anarchist. I've interviewed Mr. Rosa.'

'Something or someone I would never have in the house!' I replied stiffly.

Miss Royce laughed again, from the verandah hammock in which she had ensconced herself, with a plate of Monsieur Didier's madeleines and, I noticed, *Melbourne and Mars*. I wished her joy of it—I had work to do. The day went on, baking heat, the milk going sour, and Job returning and giving notice.

'Is this one of your Australian walking-abouts?' I asked. I had heard of such things during my two years in the colony but was new chum enough never to have encountered it before.

His face assumed an expression I had seen before. It usually meant trouble coming, in the ostler line of things: a horse was in a kicking mood, or a wheel was about to come off the trap.

'It's these hills,' he finally said. 'What they're called.'

'They're called Easter,' I said. A sere little breeze had arisen, sending a scatter of dried gum leaves dancing on the gravel path.

'You call 'em that,' he said, drawing a line in the gravel with one bare black toe. I saw his determination and let him go down the drive. At the gate he turned and called:

'I'll be back, if there's a job for me.'

Two steps on, he turned again, with a parting shot. ''Nother thing. Somebody's coming.'

'What does he mean?' said the wife, appearing with a basket to cut what flowers were in the garden, though they were fast tending to dry arrangements.

'Customers, I hope.'

Miss Joyce, from her hammock, raised one eyebrow. 'He sounded ominous.'

'Don't care, so long as they pay,' I muttered.

Thankfully she did not laugh, but merely returned to *Melbourne and Mars*.

***

Night came, with a cold collation, since Didier had a headache. The guests scattered to their rooms, fanning themselves, with moths forming a pattern of silhouettes against the muslin curtaining. I stayed on the verandah in a deck chair, smoking my cigar and listening to the soft, busy noises of a warm bush night. The bird they called the Tawny Frogmouth, like a sawn-off owl, sat on a tree branch and watched me.

Then all of a sudden it happened, a whoosh, a trail of fire across the sky, passing over Hazelmere and down into the valley. The frogs stopped pobble-bonking in the dam and the frogmouth flapped away. The wife came to our bedroom window, voluminous as the curtains in her nightgown.

'That's not Archy setting off fireworks for his Chinese feasts again?'

'No,' came a voice from the darkness beyond the verandah. 'Something much bigger.'

I turned my head, towards the plinth where the telescope stood. My eyes taking their time adjusting, I did not immediately see Miss Joyce in her dinner-dress sitting on the ground beneath the telescope.

'My legs gave way from the astonishment,' she said coolly.

I went over and helped her to her feet, just as Mowbray made an entrance, in dressing gown and tasselled nightcap.

'What in heaven was that? Falling star?'

'Stars do not fall, in astronomy,' Miss Joyce said.

'A meteorite?'

She said something that sounded remarkably like: 'If we're lucky.' Then louder: 'It landed in the valley. Near the pine plantation, from the trajectory.'

'There's a story in that,' Mowbray said, ducking back into his room. 'For the *Argus*, or whoever pays the most.'

Miss Joyce's hand was on mine, and it trembled slightly. Whither your arch looks and laughter now? I thought, but led her to the verandah. Mowbray reappeared, dressed in haste and stuffing a notebook into his coat pocket.

'Where's that Jonah?'

'Job's given notice. I suppose you want *me* to drive down to the valley in the middle of the night.'

'Not middle anymore,' said Miss Joyce. She released my hand. 'I can pay extra for your time and trouble, but I must accompany you.'

'What the mischief does a petticoat want with a meteorite?' Mowbray said.

'Woman though I am, I have made a particular study of them,' she said simply. 'Nobody for miles can inform your journalism so well.'

'Then you will need a chaperone, young lady,' said my wife from her window.

What with the womenfolk needing to get suitably dressed, and me buckling a sleepy and reluctant horse into his harness, it was the grey of pre-dawn by the time we got down the hill to the valley. Between the trunks of the pine plantation we could see a great hole in the ground beside the racetrack, with mist or smoke arising from it. Everyone in Yarraman was awake, it seemed, and we followed a procession–children in goat-carts, maids pushing perambulators, young lovers arm in arm–towards what Miss Joyce proclaimed the impact crater.

A meteorite it most certainly was not.

***

Until the cablegrams arrived from the Old Country, none of us who witnessed the events at Yarraman had any idea our experience was shared half a world away. We had to come to our own conclusions. Mowbray started making shorthand notes immediately, pen sketches of the crash site.

They made his name, eventually, and my wife pasted them into an album. In them Miss Royce appeared as an anonymous authority, supplying the necessary astronomy. Until then I had no idea of the mysterious lights and gases that had been seen on Mars, at the opposition when our two planets are closest. I thought Opposition was loyal, and in Parliament...

We four crowded into Yarraman's little telegraph office, securing our primacy with pound notes from Miss Royce and Didier's best madeira cake, which my wife had thoughtfully packed. 'Move on, nothing to see,' the local mounted constables had declared to the crowd, a complete lie. They were chiefly concerned with securing the site, and as we left the telegraph office, the train drew in, packed with more police.

Mowbray elected to stay in Yarraman, tired but keen to report any further developments. I had my doubts about that. Even if some canal-building Martian were inside the big tin can at the centre of the crater, he surely must have been smashed or cooked by the fall to earth. My wife yawned repeatedly, and Miss Royce looked pale as her blouse, with dark shadows under her eyes. I saw it was my duty to get the womenfolk back to Hazelmere, and to their beds. Miss Royce shook her head slightly but let me help her back into the trap.

'Cheer up,' I said. 'We have the best view thanks to our elevation, and the telescope, which we can turn from the heavens to earth.'

The night might have been warm, but the day proved clear and hot from the moment the sun rose. There was a stillness in the air, as if a breath waited to be exhaled. The trap crackled over dead gum leaves on the dirt track, the only sound, for the birds seemed struck silent, not even a dawn serenade of squawks. Then, in the distance I heard a slow and steady thump-thump, receding away from the valley.

Miss Royce roused a little. 'Wallaby. Out late.' She glanced around. 'I know you are a new chum, but have you ever noticed how all the animals on these hills are much the same colour as the old trees?'

Now I too glanced at the trees and stumps as they passed. Ash-grey the trunks were, nearly black. I did not pay the comment much attention, more fool me. The events of the last few hours had taken an invisible toll, manifesting now in sore joints, and an increasing weariness. So it was that when we drove through the guesthouse gates the women shucked off their tiredness like pea-shells, and it was I who collapsed into my bed and a deep sleep.

I woke, hours later, in a tangle of sweaty sheets, with strange dreams in my head: a can opening, to reveal something worse than sardines, but I knew not what, for I ran away before I could see it. The awning had been pulled down on the verandah, but the sun shone bright as diamonds through its interstices. Outside I heard soft voices, my wife and Miss Royce:

'If you believe Mr Fraser–and there is no other book about Mars here–the Martians are human as us, but better. I fear his phantasy may be optimistic.'

My wife sighed. 'The poor man was both nervous and dreamy.'

'But progressive! He imagined a Mars both Socialist and with equality of the sexes.'

'No unsuitable attachments there?' enquired my wife.

A distinct pause, then Miss Royce said: 'My unsuitable attachment was to university education, above all astronomy.'

'Ah. Never was one for book-learning myself,' said my wife. 'Still, I read in bed, if I have time at the end of the day.'

'An excellent habit,' said Miss Royce.

'And I signed the monster petition for women's suffrage, not that my husband knows. Oh, to move to New Zealand and vote!'

I thought, from my darkness: I would never hinder you, not even from the ballot-box.

When I came out dressed, I found them on the verandah, now joined by Archy. The flooring was piled with old sacks from the stable.

'Where are the maids?' I asked. Tilly, Mary-Anne and Daisy were sturdy local farm-girls, reliable until now.

'Gone home,' said my wife. 'Said they were needed, just in case.'

'To gawk at Martian-men, you mean.'

'Oh no,' said Miss Royce. 'Tilly saw a native bear climb down from a tree, to drink from the watering-can. So dry were the leaves, his usual fare! Tilly said it was a sign.'

'Of what, for heaven's sake?'

'Do you not hear the wind?' and as she spoke a gust from Hades rattled the awnings. I understood, then. Down at the Art Gallery in Melbourne, I had seen the great painting of Black Saturday, people, animals and birds, scared and dying, trampled underfoot while fleeing conflagration. Surely a day from Hell, and a day like this.

'You can flee the fire, or fight it,' she said.

I took a breath. 'An Englishman's home is his castle.'

'Then I will show you how to defend it,' she replied.

'What a day!' I said, exasperated. 'As if tin cans from Mars were not enough...'

'You should ask the men about that,' she said, with a sideways flick of her head. I squeezed between the awnings, to find Curate Pentland, clerical collar donned despite the heat, at the telescope. Didier stood by his elbow.

'The redcoats have arrived,' he greeted me. I could see with my own naked eye the scarlet of the uniforms, the colony's finest regiment, gathering around the hole in the ground.

'Martial meets Martians,' he added. 'The God of War.'

'Ready for a scrap,' said Didier, forgetting his French accent. He rubbed his hands.

'I was an army Chaplain,' said Pentland. 'My duty is down there, to minister to the wounded.'

'Including any men from Mars?' asked Miss Royce, all ironical again.

'They too are God's creatures, for He has made everything in the universe.'

'Including the Tasmanian indigenes, Job's kin? Who met a superior force, the colonizing Europeans and so came to their sad end? Their invaders sailed in boats; our visitors have been shot across the ether between the planets, we cannot guess how.'

'That is irrelevant.'

'It most certainly is not!'

Pentand swallowed, glancing at me for help. 'We must make haste.'

'No, you can't take the horse and trap!' I cried.

'It's not a hard walk down through the bush,' said Didier. 'Done it often enough, shooting ze possums for pie.'

They left not long after, two unlikely comrades suddenly finding their nerve at the whiff of warfare. I gave them a flask of water, and Miss Royce saw them on the way with her ironic laugh.

'I would not walk in the bush today. It is too like what my father recalls of Black Saturday.'

'May God preserve them,' said the wife, who can be pious on occasions.

In fact we forgot them quickly, as Miss Royce turned pedagogue, on how colonists prepare for wildfires. She and my wife donned their stoutest skirts and the maids' boots. We collected buckets, rakes, brooms and mops, and together carried the piles of sacking down to the dam, to dampen them. Archy got the ladders out, and we two cleaned the gutters of leaves. The women swept from the paths what I was now seeing as inflammables everywhere; and Archy climbed the trees, hacksaw in mouth like a pirate, to cut off any overhanging branches. We were soon all soaked to the skin with sweat, but that moisture would not be enough to save us.

Busy as we were, we managed the occasional glance valleyward, or a peep through the telescope. I could see the regiment drawn up, in a formation, and were those gun carriages being unloaded from the train? How unlike, though we did not know it yet, the response of our Northern hemisphere compatriots to the Mars-men, the doomed Deputation with their white flag. The Australian colonists did things differently, remembering the Tasmanians, as Miss Royce had? Or, what I had heard a Queensland squatter talk of one night when drunk after dinner: the dispersals, a bloody business.

We had done what we could against conflagration; I had even given the horse water and strapped on his double saddle, so the womenfolk could flee if necessary. Now Miss Royce marshalled us in front of the verandah, a troop armed only with water in buckets and mops.

'The spot fires come first, on burning leaves carried by the wind. You must dowse them as soon as they touch ground, or the house.'

While she demonstrated with the mop, I glanced down at the dam, hoping it would hold all of us, including the horse. Miss Royce had said we could expect the local bush creatures, from wombats to snakes, to join us in the watery mud if the fire rolled over the hill to engulf Hazelmere. That was our last resort, and our last chance to live.

Down in the valley, if you read Mowbray's reports, they had other concerns: the increasingly restive soldiers, the can itself restive, showing signs of life, what sort of life nobody knew. He describes the building anticipation as the can slowly opened, then the shock as the Martians emerged.

'I had thought that these Mars-men might be red, like their planet, and had even sketched in my mind some futuristic Red Indian. I held my breath, which I slowly exhaled as the form came into view, its movement slow as if weighed down by the greater mass of our Earth, which is a larger planet than Mars.

(A detail which he could have only garnered subsequently from Miss Royce!)

'It turned towards us, revealing what I could only with the greatest charity describe as a face. All around me I heard gasps, cries of amazement and horror. Tentacles I could never have imagined in my wildest dreamings, nor the dripping salivae, the slimy brown skin. White man will always trump a brown, was the mutter of an old Colonist within earshot of me, but I had my doubts: these brown-skinned creatures had travelled between the planets, something beyond any white man.'

(Again I sensed the influence of Miss Royce.)

'I cannot say for certain who started firing, some nervous foot-soldier, or a hasty young officer. All I can say is that the shot rang out, and pandemonium ensued, more shots, and then the Martians responded.'

Up at Hazelmere we heard that first shot, and the following. We crowded around the telescope, forgetting the mops and buckets, and so it was we saw clearly the flash of light.

'Lightning,' cried Miss Royce. 'A sure sparker of bushfire.'

'Too low,' I said. 'And also, too green!' for such was my impression, which as I blinked lingered lurid still against the red of my eyelids. As we gazed down–Archy had the telescope and would not let go–we saw the redcoats rally, shooting a volley. Next the green ray struck at them again, and they fell writhing to the ground, like bull-ants burnt out of their lair. Those men at the regimental rear turned prudent and retreated, becoming a rabble as the Martian ray struck again and again at them.

Their fire reached beyond the crater, to the town and beyond, taking the roof off the Yarraman Arms in an incandescent burst, sparking a grass fire in the graveyard, and even striking at the base of the Easter Hills, the steep wooded slopes below us. The dull olive of the eucalypt met the poison green from Mars, to metamorphose into fiery orange as the bush immediately ignited. In still conditions it would have been dangerous enough, but fanned by the high wind an instant conflagration sped towards us.

Archy let go of the telescope, cursing in Chinese; my wife for the first time in our married life crossed herself; Miss Joyce actually shed a tear. Me, I felt nothing but the certainty that that small dam would soon hold us all, to drown or boil, whichever came first. I reached out for my wife's hand and held it fast, feeling the warm metal of our wedding rings.

Miss Joyce, in one of her scientific papers, has since theorised there are no trees on Mars. Nor eucalypts, that tree which is a good servant when you need to boil a billy, but a bad master with a fiery, murderous temper. Yet in Australia wildfire is capricious and can be merciful. The Martians, on their dry, cold planet, did not know that, though they were intelligent, far more than us. Certainly they had the wit to use their flamethrower with the wind blowing away from them. They did not know, nor I either, that a southerly change had been blustering up from the coast, and would suddenly alter the bushfire's course–towards the Martians in their hollow, with their tin can voyager.

We four, up at Hazelmere, had the best view of what happened: how the Apocalyptic fire abruptly changed direction, a near reverse. It struck the bush at the far end of Yarraman, escalating through the pine plantation, the trees exploding like Archy's rockets, and across the crater. We saw a Martian try to run, slow and ungainly, but I felt no pity for him.. The fire set him alight like a Roman candle, tentacles and all, and he fell in a scorched, twitching heap. Then came the explosion as the fire machine met a greater enemy, sounding loud as a thunderclap. Orange trumped Mars green, to leave only dead black.

When the town's photographers got their courage up to record events, at the insistence of Mowbray, they discovered at the centre of the crater a burnt-out can, which had survived the space journey from Mars to Earth, but not an Australian bushfire. We saw Mowbray later, when he came up to collect his bags: a conquering journalistic hero, with singed hair, and a broken arm, not his writing arm, for he got his reports in. Miss Joyce's parents arrived the next morning to collect her in a fine carriage, so glad that she had survived that an unsuitable attachment to science could be tolerated. The curate and Didier we never saw again, no doubt among the human corpses from the flames, burnt beyond recognition.

I threw the guesthouse open to visiting journalists and sightseers, playing ostler myself. Archy took over the cooking and proved a dab hand at it. We had a full house, a healthy balance sheet, and even the maids returned.

Last but not least, Job came strolling up the drive, swag on back. The horse had just bitten me, so I was more than glad to see him.

'You were right,' I said. 'Somebody did come.'

It was only at the end of that long week that I finally had the time and peace for my late night cigar on the verandah. When Job and Archy came looming out of the darkness, I passed them the cigar box. We sat there and smoked, united in what I could not put words to, but which might be called brotherhood. Invading Martians and bushfires can do that to you.

'Lucky escape, Boss,' Job finally said.

'Don't I know it!' Then something struck me. 'You said it was what these hills are called. What are they called, apart from Easter?'

'In language it means Fiery Hills. See them trees, the bark still black from the last fire? Hot day, big wind, lightning—the hills burn!'

Archy stubbed out his cigar.

Job spread out his hands. 'Long as my people 'member.'

'Longer than my people,' said Archy.

I thought: Job, why did you not tell me? Then I remembered the Tasmanians. He had no reason to do so; and I did not blame him.

I got up. 'Excuse me a moment.' I went to our bedroom, where my wife was tucked up with her bedtime reading. 'Like to vote, dear heart?' I asked.

And that is why the wife and I sold Hazelmere, to invest in a sanatarium in Te Aroha, New Zealand, a green, wet land, without bushfires.

And without Martians, I hope.

OZ is Burning

Burning Hearts

Eleanor Whitworth

Apocalyptic stories are enticing to write for their conclusive, pre-ordained endings. When this callout came on the back of our harrowing and heartbreaking summer, I was inspired to indulge in a small writerly comfort. Of course, it's also satisfying to create a journey with surprises and even a smattering of wonder. Here's to keeping our curiosity alive, and to remembering that the earth does not care for us, it is we who must care for it.

Eleanor Whitworth

OZ is Burning

Burning Hearts
by
Eleanor Whitworth

I move a little closer to my mother, but not enough to touch. It's too hot. The air in the cave is getting hard to breathe. We are far enough from the opening to be shielded from the worst of the howling grit, but still, blasts of it whip in and across our skin like a horde of stinging insects. Outside, everything is red-brown. The earth lifted into the air.

I wait until everyone is asleep then, using the wall for support, slowly stand up. My stomach cranks with hunger. I step quietly around the sleeping bodies of my family. In the food nook, I stare at the water pot wanting to gulp it down, wanting to pour it over my parched body. Using all my will power, I take three small sips and carefully place it back where it was.

I lift the lid from the moss pot and remember how, when fire had reached across the horizon burning our home, we had fled for safety. After months of walking, when we first stumbled upon this cave, all I could do was carve this lid out of the gourd, slaking away the journey, the things we had seen, the things we were lucky to survive.

The pot is empty except for the small collection of dried fibres nestled in the bottom. We used to harvested it in handfuls, scraping it from the back walls. But the spring that bubbled up and moistened the grey rock is drying out. Putting the lid back, I peer into the small holes I pushed through the body of the next pot. Three ragged roaches sit listlessly, barely moving their antennae. Grandma's determined fingers can't be quick if there's nothing to catch. I decide to rest and imagine I'm eating a feast of roasted yams, their soft flesh, sweet and warm, passing down my throat, filling my stomach.

Back when the spring flowed, the yams grew. We tended a patch of them just inside the entrance of the cave, trying to hide them from the odd pair of passing eyes. The last time we had a visitor, he hurt us as he tried to take everything. We would have given him food, if he'd given us a chance. Instead, he left my uncle injured and fever-filled for days. The man ended up on the ground, colouring it with blood, my grandparents standing over him, their foraged blades dripping. We'd looked around at each other as the deep smell of him rose up making our stomachs grumble. "No," my mother had said, "we don't do that." We buried him and pushed the bloodied earth up around our yam stems.

***

I must have curled up and fallen asleep, because when I open my eyes, I find my grandfather staring at me, sad and tender. He smiles a toothless grin in spite of the sorry state of us. He clears his throat. It's story time. I sit up, loving his tales of a world ago. Of animals that hopped on two huge legs and a curved tail, of birds that sang like ringing laughter, of creeks full of fish and frogs. Of rows of houses and how water flowed when you turned a handle. This time, he tells us about the magic seats that carried your shit away. "Woosh," he said, letting the word whirl around us. Then, he lets out a fart and we laugh and hold our noses and shoo him away even though there's nowhere to go. As he turns to look out at the rotten sky, his smile turns to pain. I know that he is thinking of this ancient land, of how those who were here first should have been heeded when there was still time. How then, maybe, the land would have kept its red heart in the right place, not blown up and out to spread across the entire earth.

As quickly as it came, the storm is gone. It's deadly quiet. My mother goes to the food. She is scrupulous in her distribution. No-one ever argues. We eat our tiny portions, careful not to look at one another.

As I grind the last shred of moss between my teeth, a screech cuts into the cave like space is breaking apart. We're all up and going to look, despite the danger. I screw up my eyes against the light. A group of birds, maybe 10 of them, flap through the sky, the underside of their wings flashing blinding white, a curl of yellow feather points from their heads to the heavens. They scream like heralds. "Cockatoos!" my grandfather cries. These are the first birds I have ever seen.

I am still staring at them as they disappear off toward the horizon when my grandmother grips my arm and starts stamping. I look down to see a run of roaches skittling into the cave. We all stamp with her in a mad dance, but the roaches are mostly too fast like new life has been breathed into them. The air vibrates. My hair lifts off my head, but there is no sound of howling wind. A shadow falls over us. I look up and grab my mother's hand.

A huge, smooth, round shape hovers over us. Colours brighter than the sun flash and turn. My grandfather smiles and murmurs, "Just like in the movies."

The ship lands softly on the empty earth. A door appears, out of it come little creatures, the same shape as us, only they are all small, like me. They glow, like a fire burns inside each of their bodies. They look strong, like they are forged of the molten metal I have heard about, the scraps of which we use as blades. They gurgle at us.

My grandfather and grandmother step forward, sticky roach bodies still squirming between my grandmother's fingers.

The creatures all take a little box from the side of their bodies and eat them. Then one of them speaks.

Greetings. We are the galactic cleaners. Your time has come. The damage to your planet is too great. You no longer have your own decomposers: the flies and maggots and mushrooms are gone. So, we are here to fix that for you.

"But we are surviving," my grandfather says.

Not for long. What you are and what you do no longer matters. Everything: the good, the bad, the weak, the strong, will die. We come now because we prefer it when the flesh is fresh.

And with that, they lift their hands and their bodies light up even brighter. We look at each other as an ache spreads out from our hearts. The ache turns to heat, white heat, hotter than bare feet on exposed sand, hotter than a hand in the fire. We cry out in fear and then pain and then a strange awe as our hearts burn, and as everything, everything everywhere and everyone we know is aflame. At least now, as we burn, we also know that there is still life out there amongst the shining stars.

Harvest

Narrelle M. Harris

I'm not myself much of a gardener, but I know that we need to cultivate the philosophies and behaviour we hope to see flourish in the world. The ideas of reaping what you sow, and reaping the whirlwind, apply to how the world ends up in its parlous position at the start of "Harvest", as well as what happens to the survivors.

Narrelle M Harris

Harvest
by
Narrelle M. Harris

Anika planted the first seeds on the last day of the apocalypse. Over the last five years, the apocalypse had built momentum in spurts: a coal seam fire exploding here, a torrential three-week flood there; here a drought; there a cyclone; everywhere an isolated crisis.

When the world finished tallying the sodden, wind-wrecked, parched, burning or already ash 'isolated incidents', it realised that the beginning of the end had already reached a peak.

Declining air and water quality contributed to a respiratory pandemic, overwhelming services that did their best but failed. Just before the city riots began, toppling mobile phone towers and fracturing infrastructure in general, Anika took her dog Banjo, her backpack, water flasks and filters, and all the seeds she could salvage from her drought-perished garden, and began walking.

She left her now useless phone behind. She knew the way, and playing Farmville had never been satisfying anyway.

***

"What are you doing?" the old man asked. He was weathered as a tree, with a squint like a half-split pistachio, like his eyelids were too judgemental to let more light in.

"Being an optimist," Anika said.

"With my front lawn?"

Anika, the old man, and Banjo regarded the patchwork lawn. Anika had dug up a spot that was vivaciously green, where the water pipes underneath had ruptured and not been fixed. They never would be now. People needed functioning councils and services, and things had stopped functioning about the same time everyone realised the end had arrived while they were busy making other plans.

"Leave what I've planted for 80 days and it'll be worth your while."

"Will it now?"

"For you, your family and your neighbours."

The old fellow sighed. "The grandkids were arrested at the last big climate rally. The one that was hit by the superstorm. Don't know where they are now. Hospital. Prison, maybe." He didn't name the other option. "Maybe they got out before the floods."

"I'm sorry."

"The neighbours have all buggered off to the coast, trying to get a ship out. It's just me left now. God knows where they think they're going. The rest of the world is just as bad. Maybe they think Greta will let them into Sweden."

"You never know."

"Last I heard before the mobile network went down was that four ships sank off the Gold Coast in a hurricane or typhoon or whatever."

"That's what I heard."

The old man held his hand out to Banjo, then scratched the big dog's head.

"Not much of a guard dog."

"Do I need guarding from you?"

"Nah." He squinted at the dug-up oblong of earth. "What am I supposed to do with this?"

"Let it grow. Spare some water for it when you can, but don't let it get too wet. It should drain well here, if it ever rains again, but between the leaking pipe and the shade, they should grow all right."

"And in 80 days?"

"You harvest."

He shrugged. He offered his hand. "Name's Eric."

"Anika," she said, shaking on it. "See you!"

"You're off?"

"Places to be," she said, and meant it.

"Will I see you again?"

"Maybe," she said.

Anika whistled for her dog and started walking again.

***

From the first day, Anika had planted seeds. Pumpkins and peas. Beans and beets. Carrots and cucumbers. She planted on raised beds, over a layer of stone to aid drainage for the if-and-when of sudden downpours, fierce but never lasting. Not only vegetables but lavender, native rosemary and daisies for the precious, dwindling bees. Where the ground seemed ripe for it, where the balance of shade, sun and water was promising, Anika buried seeds and left them to grow, hoping they'd be found by a fellow gardener. Where she found edible plants growing wild, she harvested enough food for herself and a handful of seeds for the next leg of the journey. She left the rest behind for any who might follow.

Anika left potential directions in the soil, planting her hope in careful rows and loops. If any survivors were patient enough to wait, hopeful enough to tend the tiny gardens they found, the little green sprouts would spell out her destination.

HARBOUR FARM, 3442

As long as the gardener knew the place, or could get hold of a road directory, they'd find her. She planted the seeds and hoped for discovery from those with a little patience, who could make a little effort.

Anika had worked at Harbour one year while the apocalypse sneaked up on everyone, learning permaculture, agroforestry, and do-nothing Fukuoka farming methods. Her uncle had called her a raving green leftie, though he possibly meant it fondly.

Poor, dead sod.

***

Anika saw very few people as she walked. Rural Victoria had mostly emptied out in the direction of the cities, the coasts, the refugee ships, long before.

But just as Anika walked towards hope in what used to be the state's breadbasket, not everyone had abandoned the land. The smouldering world still sheltered hunters as well as gatherers.

While Anika was sleeping among the gnarled roots of a scorched and long-dead Moreton Bay fig tree, Banjo growled.

Anika's eyes opened onto a dark shadow moving among the black skeletons of a largely gum and tea-tree woodland.

"Call your dog off," came a voice.

"Why would I do that?"

"I'll shoot it." The shadow grew a long, thin arm. Barrel-shaped.

"Banjo, heel."

Banjo came to heel. The shadow resolved itself into a gaunt young man with a dirty beard. He held a shotgun.

"Get up."

"I don't think so."

"I'll shoot you."

"You won't get what you want if you shoot me."

"And what do I want, bitch?"

"Food. Water. Safety."

"And you can give that to me?"

"Sure. You see that dirt I've dug up by the tree roots? I've planted things to eat there. If you're patient and look after it, the garden will feed you, and it'll show you how to get more."

"Seriously?"

"Seriously."

"When?"

"Give it 80 days."

"About two and a half months."

"That's right."

"What am I supposed to do in the bloody meantime?"

"Cultivate patience and optimism."

"The fuck?" The man lowered the barrel of the shotgun. "You're shittin' me."

"I shit you not," said Anika earnestly. "Make sure nothing digs it up. Give it a little water, not too much. Maybe put some water out in a dish for the bees, in case they come."

"Bees."

"In case they come."

"I don't like bees."

"Don't be mean to the bees. We starve without them. As you may have noticed."

He had.

"Name's Dan". He sat in front of Anika, barring her way so that she couldn't run. Banjo sprawled between him and

Anika, casting him distrustful, judgemental looks. When Dan put out his hand to pat the dog, Banjo growled.

"I don't like your dog," Dan said, pointing his rifle at Banjo's ribs.

"He doesn't like you either. And if you shoot him, and if you hurt me, you'll never last the 80 days to fresh food."

Dan's mulish pout suggested he thought it a fair trade. The barrel of his rifle moved between Anika's chest and Banjo's, with intent to intimidate. Anika maintained her calm façade.

"Want some water?" she offered. "I've sweetened it with some wild berries I found."

He snatched the offered flask.

"Slowly," suggested Anika.

Dan guzzled it down and pulled a face. "Tastes weird."

"That'll be the berries," she explained.

He was still writhing in pain, sheened in cold sweat, fighting imaginary bees, when she hefted her backpack onto her shoulders. She sipped from her small second canteen, poured a fair measure of it onto the prospective vege patch, and slipped away, Banjo at her side.

She hoped Dan would recover from the *Atropa belladonna*. She'd made it weak, to be used only as a precaution, but he really should have sipped.

***

What with digging and planting and watering and odd conversations with strangers, it took a month for Anika and Banjo to reach Harbour Farm in the old 3442 postcode of Victoria. Postcodes, like council services, were a thing of the past. Coordinates might have been more accurate, but without functioning GPS, that wasn't much use to the average amateur horticulturalist.

Gwyn and Hettie welcomed her to Harbour.

"We were worried you wouldn't make it." Their last message had been sent a day before the mobile towers were vandalised.

"I had some things to do on the way," said Anika. "Seeds to plant. Weeds to pull."

Gwyn nodded. "We've had some tilling and sowing to do ourselves."

"I've had an idea for the gates," said Anika. "If you think it's all right."

***

Eric arrived 80 days plus walking time after Anika had left him, his rescued grandson Aaron at his side with a mud-and-ash-caked garden trolley full of seedlings. Eric's assiduously tended front lawn had provided a crop and its message. Eric eagerly learned how to cultivate tomatoes in the hydroponic shed. Aaron was more of a beans man.

Hai, Danh and their children Luke, Nam and baby Ngan arrived a fortnight later, with cuttings and seeds for choy sum, pak choy, Vietnamese mint, okra, basil, bitter melon. Stanley and Di arrived with their mustard seeds and a hopeful avocado. Lily brought a grevillea and the makings of a wooden hive box to take better care of the bees. Lowanna and Koen only stayed for a few days, sharing knowledge and swapping seeds before taking a negotiated share of the Harbour harvest back to their own mob's land near Bendigo.

The boy who drank the nightshade water never came. Anika hoped it was because he was too impatient to help the garden to grow.

Every few weeks, new people came, in response to the budding maps Anika had planted. They came into Harbour like dandelions on the wind. Others found Harbour without the vegetable signpost.

Anika had woven the passionfruit vines through the wires and wood of the farm gate: the left side spelled REAP in stems during the winter and in leafy, floral abundance when the spring came; the right spelled SOW.

The hungry, thirsty, angry woman at the gate objected to the flowery sign. "That's the wrong way 'round," she said. "You sow, and then you reap."

"Yes," agreed Anika. "And what you plant determines what you grow."

"You've got fresh food. I want some."

"We're happy to share. Come in."

The woman walked with Anika through the gates. Banjo bounded out from where he'd been guarding the new chickens. So far, not a single chick had been whisked away by falling oak leaves, and Banjo strutted with canine pride.

"How did you find us?" Anika asked.

"I'm from around Wartook way," she said. "I visited this farm once. I thought it might still be here. So I walked."

Her shoes were ragged, and her legs blackened from the ash. Wartook had been burned to cinders in the last great Grampians conflagration, still smouldering and flaring up every few months. Nobody knew how there was anything left to burn.

"We'll feed you, then you can help farm, learn some techniques, take some seeds and seedlings with you if you want to leave after that," offered Anika.

"And if I don't wanna work?"

"We won't let you starve," said Anika.

Anika showed the woman, named Audrey, around the farm and its self-contained ecosystem. They watched Eric and Danh bury a deformed, stillborn calf in the composting area far downwind of the farmhouses.

"Poor little thing." Audrey's hostility had drowned in the flask of filtered creek water Anika had provided. She ate a tomato straight from the vine and almost cried at the strong, sweet tang; nearly wept for the memory of everyone who had been forcibly evacuated from the Grampians. After that, she'd struck out on her own.

"We're still getting birth defects in the livestock," Anika noted. "But none of them go to waste. We give them back to the soil. Blood and bone is good compost."

Audrey stayed and planted pumpkins and radishes. She planted hopes and grew friends.

***

Lachlan, too, reaped what he sowed, when he came to Harbour.

"Just give me what I want and I'll go." He used a rifle for emphasis. The farm lost a good laying hen when he demonstrated that it was loaded and he was prepared to use it.

"Attenborough will have to go in the compost," noted Audrey ruefully.

"I'll put *you* in the fucking compost. Load my truck."

Nobody asked how he'd got hold of the petrol.

"How are we supposed to plant again next season if you take it all?" asked Gwyn.

"Not my problem."

"It will be next year when you're hungry and we haven't anything for you to take," Eric pointed out.

"There are other farms. I'll be right."

Anika sighed and pinched the bridge of her nose. Beside her, Banjo whined and pressed against her leg.

"I'll shoot your fucking dog, too, if you don't get a wriggle on."

"Hold your horses," soothed Eric. "We don't want trouble."

"Load. The Fucking. Truck."

Gwyn sent Eric and Aaron to get the crate of freshly harvested carrots and potatoes; Danh and the kids went to fetch the corn seed stock. Hai took on the collection of the eggs and to find crates for the chickens. Audrey cried as she put a halter on their cow.

Hettie had to hold onto Banjo's collar as Lachlan forced Anika at gunpoint into the main farmhouse, which was built into the side of a hill. Better insulation in summer and winter; protection from fire. Not from bushrangers, though

Anika's hands shook. "What do you want?"

"I want you to empty your fridge."

"We don't have a fridge. No electricity, remember?"

"You know what I fucking mean."

She knew what he fucking meant. She opened the door to the pantry they'd dug deeper into the side of the hill. She went into the cool, damp dark while Lachlan stood in the kitchen with his rifle.

She returned with a jug of water in one hand. Balanced on the other arm was a wooden box filled with their few jars of preserved produce. A small wheel of just-matured camembert rested across the lids.

"You ripper!" Lachlan snatched the cheese and bit a chunk right out of it. The white centre oozed and stuck to the roof of his mouth. His grabby hand snatched for the water jug. Anika didn't resist.

Lachlan tipped the open jug right back, necking it like a pub brew. "This tastes funny."

"It's sweetened with wild berries," she said. "It's better if you sip it."

Lachlan took another bite of ripe, soft cheese and washed it down with gulps from the jug.

***

Audrey insisted that Attenborough the chicken be composted in a separate heap to Lachlan, even though it wasn't the best use of resources. Everything went back to the earth in the end. The cruel compost exactly the same as the kind, though not nearly as often.

A Town Called Hope

Silvia Brown

This story is dedicated to Chris Cokley. A close friend that gifted me his drawing of a red-faced girl with dark blue hair and striking features. He said there was a story to her and that it was up to me to figure it out. The drawing remained over my desk, her staring eyes reminding me of the work to be done. Early last year we lost Chris to a sudden accident in Hawaii and his drawing became even more valuable. But I couldn't get myself to write about it then. It wasn't until the fires devastated Australia that it came to me, as I was writing a story to be donated to an anthology to support the firefighters, Stories of Hope. A short, tense race against time in a near future where the next generation has evolved in ways we cannot comprehend. H is the girl on the drawing. Her red skin glows when she feels the fire coming closer and her hair turns an eerie shade of blue. She may be an outcast to most but she could well be our last hope.

Chris' drawing can be found on Instagram: https://www.instagram.com/p/BMVlP6Ggjcb/

Silvia Brown

OZ is Burning

A Town Called Hope
by
Silvia Brown

Legend tells of a summer of flames, generations ago, when nature gave up on us. The land has not stopped burning since, no matter how hard fireys like my father work to keep it at bay.

Growing up, he dragged us all over the country, looking for a safe place.

"Nowhere is safe," he said. My mother covered my ears, but it was already too late. I'd heard him and he knew what to do. I saw the spark of determination back in his eyes. That night he packed his bag and left for a place called Hope. Mother chose not to believe him, and we stayed with the latest community we'd found.

I'd wanted to believe him, with all I had. A year later, I lay on the grass next to my bike and wondered if Hope was also the stuff of legend. Maybe the hazy smoke that turned the sky red, and tainted my skin the same hue, was at fault. Maybe I was the one to blame for my father's absence.

Setting my hand on the ground, I sat up and felt the familiar rush of the roaring blaze that consumes everything in its path. The feeling came over me as it always did, making me feel claustrophobic in my own body. My blood singing as the same flames burnt with the pulse of the approaching inferno. The conflicting sensations of thrill and shame surged through me. This is why Mother and the rest are afraid of me. Filled with unstoppable energy, I grabbed my bike and started pedalling. Riding through the dense smoke knowing I couldn't stop. Not until I got home, not until I joined Mother and the others in the safety of the underground wildfire bunker.

My legs ached by the time I jumped off my bike and ran to the entrance, grabbing for a handle that would not give, no matter how hard I tried.

"No!" I screamed. The fire was getting closer, I could feel it taking over me. Back on my bike, I raced to the gravel road, going as fast as I could, fleeing from the wall of fire approaching behind me.

A sudden wind change turned the fire and gave me the chance I needed to escape. I rode until I started panting and the next farm emerged through the red twilight. I'd decided to keep going when I saw her. A young woman in black clothing returning to the house. I had to warn her. Taking the path onto the property, I dropped my bike by the porch and walked inside. There was no one in the hall, my heart pounding in my chest. I knew I'd seen her.

The kitchen was also deserted, and my throat ached at the sight of the tap. I ran it until the water came out in a clear, steady stream. I drank greedily and filled my bottle until the stream went dry. They'd run out of water and I knew that was a death sentence.

From where I stood, I noticed a pantry door and my tummy rumbled at the thought of food. As I got closer, I heard chewing noises coming from inside. I yanked the door open. A boy, that by his looks and his size, could have been my little brother, his skin the same strange red hue as mine. His cheeks were full of the bread he cradled to his chest. His startled scream was muffled by his mouthful and he coughed it all out, gasping for air.

We stared at each other and his skin began to glow. He felt the approaching fire too. We needed to find the woman and get out of there, there was no time to lose.

"Where is she? The woman? Is she your mother? We have to go!" I yelled.

He looked down and grabbed onto his knees, hiding his face.

"They're gone. Mum... she said... 'You'll be safe here,' that's what she said. I wish she'd lock me in so you wouldn't have found me. I wish she'd taken me with her, but I'm not one of them. Please just let me be. Lock me up. So she'll know where to find me when they all rise to meet the lord saviour."

You gotta be kiddin' me, I thought to myself. I had to think and fast.

"I know you can feel it too," I said, and he lifted his head, a surprised and guilty expression on his face.

"But Mum said it's better this way, there's something wrong with me."

"Me too."

The roar of the fire drowned out his reply, I grabbed his hand.

"My father is a firey! He'll take care of us!" I yelled. Or at least so I hoped.

The boy held on and we went outside to get my bike.

The farm was ablaze, cutting off our escape. "Do you have a bike?!" I asked.

He nodded and ran to the end of the porch, grabbing a kid's bike with training wheels. *Oh, Christ*, I thought as he came rushing back and looked up at me expectantly.

The peeling paint on the porch began to char in the searing heat. The building creaked, as the burning structure weakened over our heads.

"I'm Eli!" he shouted, cleaning his face with his sleeve.

"Not now!" I screamed back at him, gesturing towards the road. "Go!"

I got off the porch and on my bike before the house could collapse on us. Eli got on his own right behind me.

We charged through the wall of flames, the fire curling around us until our clothes smouldered and our bike tires started to melt.

On the other side we started pedalling, our skin glowing like hot embers.

"My mother always called me H," I said as we biked down the road.

"What does it stand for?" Eli followed me closely, his legs pumping as he tried to keep up. I didn't answer because I didn't know.

***

At the top of a hill we stopped and drank some water while I checked my father's map. The one thing he'd left me with. A circle marked the place called Hope and, some distance below it, an 'X' with the words, *'Fire Station'* in his handwriting.

"We have to keep going until we get here," I said pointing at the fire station.

"How much longer?" Eli asked and I shrugged.

The wind changed and I raised my hand, feeling the bushfire being pushed towards us. Eli looked at me with wide eyes and started riding ahead.

***

As the sun went down, our water dwindled but not our determination. We kept going, following the scorched signs that guided us towards a red brick building that the map said should be my father's fire station.

There were fire trucks parked outside and we tried to open the taps for water without success. I walked around the structure, looking for a way in, Eli trailing behind me.

"Can I help you?" a man's voice boomed. He was wearing ragged, yellow uniform pants and big, black boots. A bushy beard covered his face.

My shoulders felt lighter, he'd know where to find my father. As he got closer to us, I stopped and so did he.

"H!" He fell to his knees and I ran towards him. Just like I'd daydreamed every day since he'd left. His arms embraced me while Eli caught up.

I let go of my father and introduced him.

"Dad, this is Eli. He's from a farm just a few blocks from us."

"Hi, matey," Dad said before going on, "H, where's your mother?"

"I was late." Tears streamed from my eyes. "I was playing outdoors when I felt the fire coming... and they, they locked me out of the bunker."

My father frowned and asked me no more questions. Eli avoided his gaze, probably thinking about how his mother had abandoned him too.

"Not to worry, Munchkin," my father said, and I was embarrassed and delighted. It had been a long time since he'd called me by my pet name. "I'll take care of you. Both of you."

***

Riding in the firey's truck with my father and Eli, I kept an eye out for the sign for Hope but it never came. Had I missed it perhaps?

"Dad, are we there yet?" I asked.

Eli looked up, his eyes asking the same question.

"Not quite, we need to pick up the brigade on the way," he explained.

Clicking a switch, he turned the sirens on and Eli buzzed with excitement. Soon enough we saw torchlights coming out of the dark bush. Firemen climbed on our truck as they took a break from the fight. My eyes felt sticky and I struggled to keep them open. I woke up when the truck stopped.

I followed my father into an enormous fire station, twice the size of the one before. That was when I first noticed how ragged his uniform was. How thin the soles of his boots were. The crisp stench of burnt leather strong in the filtered air. He led us to a room with long tables filled with more firemen. Their uniforms were just like my father's. Their faces stained black with soot, their eyes aching red, and the moment they saw us, the room fell silent.

"Dad," I asked, grabbing his sleeve. "Is this Hope?"

"No, Munchkin," he replied. I looked at him, confused.

"My father was a firefighter and so was his father before him. They knew there is no such place. Fighting alongside my brothers, I learnt that hope is not about safety. Not about defeating an impossible enemy. Hope is persevering against the odds and never giving up the fight. Hope, is the future. H, you are Hope."

About the Authors

Alma Alexander is a novelist, short story writer and anthologist whose work has appeared in over a dozen languages and on every continent save Antarctica. She lives in the cedar woods of America's Pacific Northwest with her husband, the obligatory two writer's cats, and assorted visiting wildlife.

Paula Boer loves wildlife and wildernesses, and writes fiction and non-fiction about nature. She is passionate about all animals, even snakes and spiders, and has a particular love of fungi. She and her dog live on 500 acres, primarily of forest, which was devastated in the January 2020 bushfire. When not writing, Paula cares for the recovering wildlife, including kangaroos, wallabies, and wombats. Cockatoos and other parrots are frequent visitors to her bird table.

Paula's *Brumbies* series of novels for horse lovers is set in her home area of the Snowy Mountains of Australia. Her fantasy horse trilogy, *The Equinora Chronicles*, is set in a land ruled by unicorns, complete with dragons and other magical creatures, where humans are secondary to equines.

Paula can be found on FaceBook at Paula.Boer.3 and PaulaBoerAuthor, plus via her websites www.paulaboer.com and www.brumbiesnovels.com. Her novels, published by IFWG Australia in both paperback and e-book, are available at major online bookstores such as Amazon.

Silvia Brown (née Silvia Cantón Rondoni) is a Spanish-born Australian horror writer and poet. Silvia lived and worked in Ireland, Canada, The Netherlands, (and Melbourne) before moving to Canberra to focus on her writing. Her current projects include a poetry collection, a few short story commissions and a literary translation.

Silvia enjoys long naps with her bulldog Patch and attending writing conventions.

Sue Bursztynski lives in Melbourne, where her day job for many years was teacher librarian at a state secondary school. This has come in handy over the years when she needed beta readers. Most of her writing has been for children and teens, including books, short fiction and articles. Her YA fantasy novel *Wolfborn* was a Notable book in the Children's Book Council of Australia awards. She has also been published in *Andromeda Spaceways,* Ford Street anthologies and a number of fantasy anthologies. She reads slush for a speculative fiction semiprozine.

Sue has a book blog, The Great Raven, at https://suebursztynski.blogspot.com, where she posts regularly about fiction, mostly fantasy and SF.

Jack Dann has written or edited over seventy-five books, including the international bestseller *The Memory Cathedral*, *The Rebel*, and *The Silent*. He is a recipient of the Nebula Award, the World Fantasy Award (two times), the Australian Aurealis Award (three times), the Chronos Award, the Darrell Award for Best Mid-South Novel, the Ditmar Award (five times), the Peter McNamara Achievement Award and also the Peter McNamara Convenors' Award for Excellence, the Shirley Jackson Award, and the *Premios Gilgames de Narrativa Fantastica* award. He has also been honored by the Mark Twain Society (Esteemed Knight).

His most recent short story collection is *Concentration*. Critic and scholar Marleen Barr wrote: "Dann is a Faulkner and a Márquez for Jews. His fantastic retellings of the horror stories Nazis made real are more truth than fantasy."

His latest novel is *Shadows in the Stone*. Kim Stanley Robinson called it "such a complete world that Italian history no longer seems comprehensible without his cosmic battle of spiritual entities behind and within every historical actor and event." Forthcoming is a Centipede Press *Masters of Science Fiction* volume.

Dr. Dann is an Adjunct Senior Research Fellow in the School of Communication and Arts at the University of Queensland.

Harold Gross spent several years commuting to and working in Melbourne, but now lives in the mountains outside of Seattle, Washington in the US. During his time in Australia, he fell in love with Melbourne, its food, and its people. He's still friends with many who lived through the fires that swept across the continent so recently.

His efforts, solo and collaborative (with Eve Gordon as Gordon Gross), have been published on three continents (North America, Europe, Australia) in such venues as Fantasy & Science Fiction, Analog, Pseudopod, Aeon, and Story Seed Vault. Other stories have appeared in anthologies as varied as Star Trek: Strange New Worlds III and even a cookbook. Currently he has stories in B-Cubed's Alternative Truths: Endgame and on HybridFiction.net. He's received several prizes in various fiction contests and an honourable mentions in *The Year's Best Fantasy & Horror*.

A near-daily blog of spoiler-free movie reviews (2300+) can be found at his website: http://www.haroldgross.com or follow him on Twitter: @haroldgross.

Narrelle M Harris writes crime, horror, fantasy, romance and erotica. Her 30+ novels and short stories have been published in Australia, US and the UK.

Award nominations include *Fly By Night* (Ned Kelly Awards), *Witch Honour* and *Witch Faith* (short-listed for the George Turner Prize), and *Walking Shadows* (Chronos Awards; Davitt Awards). Her ghost/crime story *Jane* won the Athenaeum Library's "Body in the Library" prize at the 2017 Scarlet Stiletto Awards. In 2020, *Scar Tissue and Other Stories* was nominated for the 2019 Aurealis Awards for Best Collection.

Her work includes vampire novels, erotic spy adventures, paranormal thrillers, het and queer romance, traditional Holmesian mysteries, and Holmes/Watson romances *The Adventure of the Colonial Boy* (2016) and *A Dream to Build a Kiss On* (2018). Her 2019 releases included spec-fic het romance, *Grounded*, the *Scar Tissue and Other Stories* collection, and rock 'n roll urban fantasy adventure, *Kitty and Cadaver*. Some of the songs from that novel are being recorded and performed by Melbourne band, Bronze.

On Patreon, Narrelle is writing novellas in the Duo Ex Machina M/M romance crime series. The fifth novella, Little Star is being serialised in 2020.

https://www.patreon.com/NarrelleMHarris

See more at www.narrellemharris.com.

Jared Kavanagh is a writer of alternate history, speculative fiction and sometimes just plain weird stuff. He lives in Sydney, Australia with his wife and two daughters, all of whom are kind enough to let him take some time away from them now and then to get some writing done.

He is the author of the *Lands of Red and Gold* alternate history series together with several short stories in anthologies from Sea Lion Press.

He has tried over seventy day jobs in his life, none of which lasted longer than a couple of years. His record for shortest job was one which lasted three hours. The job had been offered as graphic design, but it was really data entry. So he took an early lunch break and never came back.

No matter what other jobs he has tried, he always ends up returning to writing. You can keep up with Jared on Facebook: https://www.facebook.com/jkavanaghauthor/

E.E. King is a painter, performer, writer, and biologist—She'll do anything that won't pay the bills, especially if it involves animals.

Ray Bradbury called her stories, "marvelously inventive, wildly funny and deeply thought-provoking. I cannot recommend them highly enough."

King has won numerous various awards and fellowships for art, writing, and environmental research.

She's been published widely. Her books include Dirk Quigby's Guide to the Afterlife.

King was the founding Director of the Esperanza Community Housing's Art & Science Program, worked as an artist-in-residence in Los Angeles, San Francisco, Sarajevo and the J. Paul Getty Museum's and Science Center's Arts & Science Development Program.

Her landmark mural, A Meeting of the Minds (121' x 33') can be seen on Mercado La Paloma in Los Angeles. King has also painted murals in Cuenca, Spain and in Tuscany, Italy.

She's worked with children in Bosnia, crocodiles in Mexico, frogs in Puerto Rico, egrets in Bali, mushrooms in Montana, archaeologists in Spain, butterflies in South Central Los Angeles, lectured on island evolution and marine biology on cruise ships in the South Pacific and the Caribbean, painted murals in Los Angeles and Spain.

Check out paintings, writing, musings and books at -- www.elizabetheveking.com
eviekng@gmail.com

Lauren E. Mitchell lives on traditional Wurundjeri land (Melbourne) with their husband and cats. They've been writing as long as they can remember. Their preferred genres are fantasy, horror, and the supernatural, although in today's uncertain world they're not quite as big on apocalyptic fiction as they once were. Lauren won the 2014 ASFF Amateur Writing Competition, and was a nominee for the 2018 Norma K. Hemming Award. They were the Melbourne Municipal Liaison for National Novel Writing Month for ten years, and have been on the committee for Continuum for several years. Lauren can be found on social media at twitter.com/LEBMitchell or facebook.com/laurenmitchellwrites.

Jason Nahrung grew up on a Queensland cattle property and now lives in Ballarat with his wife, the writer Kirstyn McDermott. He works as an editor and journalist to support his travel addiction. His fiction is invariably darkly themed, perhaps reflecting his passion for classic B-grade horror films and '80s goth rock. His most recent long fiction is the Gothic tale Salvage (Twelfth Planet Press) and his outback vampire duology Blood and Dus and The Big Smoke (Clan Destine Press). More than 20 of his short stories have been published, all in the speculative fiction genre, and some of his works have been finalists for awards in Australia and the US. In 2019 he was awarded a PhD in creative writing from The University of Queensland in the field of climate fiction. With his wife, he runs a monthly spoken word event in Ballarat and is active in the writing community. He lurks online at www.jasonnahrung.com

Suzanne Newnham is a writer, trance medium, health advocate, and researcher using tai chi, qigong, and meditation to manage pain. She is the author of *Ethics of a Psychic Reading* as well as numerous published short stories and articles.

From 2015, Suzanne has been writing monthly on various aspects of coping and living with chronic pain and extreme hypersensitivity to environmental factors for PnP Authors e-magazine; and since 2016 has written regularly on ethics for the International Psychics Association. She has articles published in: Traditional Medicine Research's journal 'Life Research'; spiritual magazines; and, Canberra Australia's Health Care Consumer Association. Suzanne has also co-authored four novellas: a fractured fairytale, dystopian thriller, 'who dun it' murder mystery and a romance. She is finalising publication of a biographical memoir of the first female accountant to BORAL Ltd who in 2017 was accepted into the National (Australia) Pioneering Women's Hall of Fame.

Suzanne Newnham is a member of various writing groups; pain related organisations; psychic and spiritual associations.

Eight years ago, moving with her husband to the beautiful creative-inspiring NSW South Coast fulfilled Suzanne's lifelong dream of living between mountain and sea.

https://www.suzanne-newnham.com

Dr Gillian Polack is a writer, editor, historian and teacher, with doctorates in both history and creative writing. She has over a dozen books published in Australia and overseas. Her 2019 novel, *The Year of the Fruit Cake* and was recently shortlisted for the best SF novel in the

Aurealis Awards. Her novels are mostly science fiction or contemporary fiction with fantastical elements. Several of her books have been short-listed for awards and her monograph *History and Fiction* is a standard reference in university courses. She blogs for Book View Café, the History Girls and for Medievalists.net. Gillian is an ethnohistorian and Medievalist, currently researching the critical role fiction plays in cultural transmission. In her copious spare time she practises sarcasm, cooking, reading and narrative analysis.

Ann Poore is a harpist, singer, songwriter, and poet from Melbourne, Australia. She has recently retired from Nursing.

Ann has two CD's published—"Prayer for a Peaceful Ending" and "Bullets Like Rain", both of which are available through iTunes, CDBaby, and all streaming platforms.

Aura Redwood is a writer of both comics and short stories living with her wonderful partner in Canberra, Australia.

Aura is a big geek with a great fondness for traveling, supernatural creatures and cute novelty food. She spends her free time reading, writing, gaming, and binge-watching TV shows and movies.

Clare Rhoden started writing stories as a young child, and never really stopped. She lives in Melbourne Australia with her husband and a highly intelligent poodle-cross called Aeryn. Clare is an author, blogger and book reviewer inspired by politics, culture and the march of history. Her thought-provoking stories and popular characters inspire hope and optimism through challenging times, with novels ranging from historical fiction (*The Stars in the Night*) to the dystopian world of *The Chronicles of the Pale* trilogy. You can find Clare's books, blog posts and reviews at https://clarerhoden.com

Zena Shapter writes from a castle in a flying city hidden by a thundercloud. Her writing reaches across ages and genre into the heart of storytelling. Author of *Towards White* (IFWG 2017) and co-author of *Into Tordon*

(MidnightSun 2016), she's won over a dozen national writing competitions—including a Ditmar Award, the Glen Miles Short Story Prize and the Australasian Horror Writers' Association Award for Short Fiction. Her short work has appeared in the Hugo-nominated 'Sci Phi Journal', 'Midnight Echo' as well as their Australian Shadows Awarded 'best of' anthology, 'Antipodean SF' and Award-Winning Australian Writing (twice). Reviewer for Tangent Online Lillian Csernica has referred to her as a writer who "deserves your attention". She's a movie buff, keen traveler, story nerd, and inclusive creativity advocate, who's founded community creativity projects for writers such as the 'Art & Words Project' and the award-winning Northern Beaches Writers' Group. She's also a writing mentor, editor, book creator, HSC English tutor, Service NSW Creative Kids Provider, and short story judge. Find her online via every major social media platform and zenashapter.com

Lucy Sussex was born in Christchurch, New Zealand. She has abiding interests in women's lives, Australiana, and crime fiction. Her award-winning fiction includes the novel, *The Scarlet Rider* (1996, reprint Ticonderoga 2015), and her anthology *She's Fantastical* was shortlisted for the World Fantasy Award. She has five short story collections. Her *Women Writers and Detectives in the Nineteenth Century* (2012) examines the mothers of the mystery genre. *Blockbuster: Fergus Hume and The Mystery of a Hansom Cab* (Text), won the 2015 Victorian Community History Award and was shortlisted for the Ngaio Marsh Award. In 2018 she was a Creative Fellow at the State Library of Victoria.

Kyla Lee Ward is a Sydney-based creative who works in many modes, which have variously garnered Stoker, Rhysling and Ditmar nominations. Her novel *Prismatic* (co-authored as Edwina Grey) won an Aurealis Award for Best Horror, and her poem "Revenants of the Antipodes" the inaugural Australian Shadow for poetry. Her short fiction has appeared in *Weirdbook, Shadowed Realms* and on gothic.net, and in the anthologies *Gods, Memes and*

Monsters: a 21st century Bestiary and *Hear Me Roar*, among others. Her work on RPGs including *Demon: the Fallen* saw her appear as a guest at Gencon Australia. Her short film, 'Bad Reception', screened at the Third International Vampire Film Festival and she is a founding member of the company responsible for *Deadhouse: Tales of Sydney Morgue* and The Theatre of Blood, which has also produced her work. She travels widely, rhymes adventurously and reacts badly to smoke. To see some very strange things, try http://www.kylaward.com.

Eleanor Whitworth Eleanor lives in Sydney with her husband and young child. Primarily a short story writer, you can find her work in various magazines, including: *Not One of Us, SQ Magazine* and *Meanjin,* and anthologies by Deadset Press and Black Hare Press. In her non-fiction world, Eleanor works as a freelance copywriter for artists, universities and Arup's foresight and innovation team. You can find her on Twitter as @elewhitworth or more backstory at eleanorwhitworth.com.

About B-Cubed Press

B Cubed Press is a small press that publishes big books about things that matter.

A percentage of EVERY book we publish is donated to Charity. Usually the ACLU. For this book we made an exception and are donating WIRES

We can be reached at Kionadad@aol.com.

Our writers gather routinely on the "B Cubed Project Page" on Facebook and we can also be found at B Cubed Press.com.

www.ingramcontent.com/pod-product-compliance
Lightning Source LLC
Chambersburg PA
CBHW020416180626
46812CB00003B/1005